Dear Romance Reader,

Welcome to a world of breathtaking passion and never-ending romance.
Welcome to *Precious Gem Romances*.

It is our pleasure to present *Precious Gem Romances*, a wonderful new line of romance books by some of America's best-loved authors. Let these thrilling historical and contemporary romances sweep you away to far-off times and places in stories that will dazzle your senses and melt your heart.

Sparkling with joy, laughter, and love, each *Precious Gem Romance* glows with all the passion and excitement you expect from the very best in romance. Offered at a great affordable price, these books are an irresistible value—and an essential addition to your romance collection. Tender love stories you will want to read again and again, *Precious Gem Romances* are books you will treasure forever.

Look for fabulous new *Precious Gem Romances* each month—available only at Wal★Mart.

Kate Duffy
Editorial Director

Anx

PURSUED

Elizabeth Jennings

Zebra Books
Kensington Publishing Corp.
http://www.zebrabooks.com

ZEBRA BOOKS are published by

Kensington Publishing Corp.
850 Third Avenue
New York, NY 10022

First Printing: April, 1999
10 9 8 7 6 5 4 3 2 1

Printed in the United States of America

This book is dedicated to the wonderful, strong women in my family—Cousin Helen, Aunt Sally, Aunt Clara—and to the memory of my beloved mother.

One

"Good morning, Miss Andersen," a small voice called out.

Julia Templeton kept on walking down the school corridor, then suddenly froze. *Sally Andersen.* That was her name now. Ever since she'd happened on a mobster finishing off one of his minions in the parking lot of a cement factory two months earlier, her life had been turned upside down. She'd been hustled from the Boston Police Department's headquarters to the U.S. Marshal's Office in a heartbeat, and the photograph she'd snapped at the moment of the hit had become a crucial piece of evidence. In the space of a few hours, she'd been spirited out of Boston and had lost her identity as Julia Templeton, rising young editor at Warwick Publishing and had been reborn as Sally Andersen, grade school teacher in Simpson, Idaho.

Would she ever get used to it? Julia didn't feel like a Sally Andersen, though she didn't know *what* she felt like anymore. She glanced down at herself, still amazed at what she saw.

She'd been a stylish dresser in her previous life. Now she wore a dark brown skirt, a dull brown sweater and sensible flat-heeled brown shoes. All of which matched the plain brown they'd insisted she dye her hair, covering the glossy red Julia had been so proud of. Witness-Protection-Program Brown, she'd called it. Idiotically, it was when she'd had to dye her hair that her predicament had truly come home to her. She had read the instructions on the box through streaming eyes—which might explain the lifeless, light-absorbing mass on top of her head. She'd cut it herself and she thought she looked like a female George Clooney.

Herbert Davis hadn't let her bring any of her own clothes. Herbert Davis. Her own U.S. Marshal. He couldn't have looked less like the part. Had she ever thought about it—which she hadn't—she would have supposed that a U.S. Marshal would have to be tall, athletic, steely-eyed, with a six-shooter strapped to his lean hips. Not short, roundish and nearsighted with a cell phone in the holster.

Davis had seen her off from Logan airport, two hours after she'd inadvertently witnessed the murder, with a suitcase full of stodgy, dull clothes she wouldn't ordinarily have been caught dead in. *Oh well,* she had thought, *I can always buy more clothes later.* She hadn't counted on the fact that the best-stocked store in Simpson, Idaho, would be Kellogg's Hardware Emporium.

Julia walked into her classroom of second-graders, then stopped as a small human cannonball barreled straight into her stomach. She let out a whoosh of air, then laid her hands on two narrow shoulders. The child's small bones felt as fragile as a bird's under her hands.

"Rafael." She smiled and hunkered down. Rafael Martinez was her favorite pupil. The shy boy had hov-

ered around her over the past two months, bringing her fistfuls of late-blooming daisies, a piece of filthy tea-colored bone he assured her was a dinosaur fossil and—her favorite—a tiny spring-green turtle.

Julia had been worried to see him growing sadder and sadder over the last four weeks. Something was happening at home. She could have resisted the temptation to interfere had Rafael become aggressive and unruly. But he had simply turned quiet, then morose, his unhappiness plain to see in his little round face.

"Hey, buddy," Julia said gently. She reached out a finger to casually wipe away a tear. "What's the matter?"

He mumbled something at the floor. She thought she heard 'Missy' and 'mother' and glanced sharply at Missy Jensen, her cropped hair and overalls making her look more like a little boy than a little girl.

"Baffroom," Rafael mumbled into her waist, head down. He needed to cry in private. Julia opened her arms, and the small boy snaked around her and rushed off to the bathroom across the hall.

She walked over to where Missy was staring after Rafael, a stricken look in her eyes.

"What was that about, Missy?" she asked quietly.

"I don't know, ma'am." The little girl's lower lip quivered. "I didn't mean nothin'. All I asked was would Rafael's momma take him trick-or-treating with me." Missy raised troubled cornflower-blue eyes. "Then he just runned away."

"Ran," Julia corrected automatically. "Well, then, just let him be. We have to get to work if we want everything ready for this evening." Julia stepped away and clapped her hands. "Okay, class, let's get going. It's Halloween and we've got Mr. Big to get ready."

All the kids had brought their own pumpkins to prepare for Halloween that evening. Fourteen small pumpkins with rather crazed, skewed grins were lined up on the shelf. Now it was time to tackle Mr. Big. One of the local farmers had dropped by that morning without a word—the inhabitants of Simpson sure weren't talkers—and with a forty-pound whopper of a pumpkin for the kids to carve.

Carving the enormous pumpkin was going to be a class project and that evening the finished product would be put out on the steps of the school, lit up with a candle.

"Okay, gang." Julia clapped her hands. "Let's get going. We've got half an hour to put the biggest, meanest jack-o'-lantern this town has ever seen on the school steps."

"Yeah! Oh boy!" In a tangle of limbs and with a maximum of fuss and mess, Mr. Big began to take shape. Oddly, the noise and confusion soothed Julia. She was used to the clamor and bustle of a big city. Simpson was silent and deserted even at noon.

She watched the kids try to scoop the seeds out of the enormous pumpkin, interfering only to pick up most of what slopped out onto the floor so the kids wouldn't skid and fall down. Jim, the janitor, would take care of the rest.

Just then, Rafael slipped inside the classroom, eyes dry but red-rimmed. Julia hoped he would join in the fun, but he stayed on the outskirts of the whirl of activity. Julia sighed, and penned another note to his parents, asking to meet with them, slipped it into the little boy's lunchbox. It was the fifth note she had sent home in two weeks. Much as she hated the thought, she would have to call his parents if she got no response this time.

"Miss Andersen, lookee."

Julia was wondering about what kind of parents Rafael had, and it took her a minute to respond to the excited request. She turned to find thirteen shiny faces turned up to her, so many small sunflowers to her sun. If they only knew she was winging it, she thought wryly.

Tongue in cheek, Julia tilted her head. "Sca-a-a-ry. Looks like something from a horror movie." Something sharp and painful tugged in her chest at the sighs of satisfaction. Her smile faded. They were so young. Being scared was fun at that age—things that go bump in the night, bogeymen leaping out of closets, and mommy and daddy ready to make them go away with a hug and a smile.

Who was going to make her bogeymen go away?

A wild, clanging noise erupted. Julia jumped at the bell and cursed her jangled nerves.

"Bye, Miss Andersen! Bye." In the space of a second or two, the room was emptied. Nature knew nothing faster than small children leaving the classroom at the end of the school day. In an amazingly short time, the whole school was deserted. It was Friday and the teachers, too, left as soon as possible.

She would see some of the children that evening, decked out in their costumes. A bag full of candy was waiting on the scuffed table next to the front door.

The silence in the school was eerie, but that was no surprise. The whole town was eerie. Simpson, Idaho, population 3,475. Almost four thousand souls, actually, if you counted Greater Metropolitan Simpson, which included the inhabitants of the ranches scattered over the wide, empty countryside.

Simpson was like the old joke: you either wanted to be there or you were lost. It didn't lead to anywhere and it wasn't on the way to anywhere.

Julia looked out the classroom window. A single tiny snowflake drifted by. It melted before it hit the ground, but one quick glance at the sky told her that there was more up there where that came from. And her boiler had chosen now of all times to get temperamental on her.

A huge lump of homesickness lay heavy in her chest. Back home, if anything had gone wrong with her heating system, she would have called the super, Joe, and it would have been fixed by the time she'd gotten home from work. Back home, on a cold, dank day like this, she'd have made a point of doing something special. Maybe rent a movie, or arrange to meet a friend for dinner. Dora, say. Dora liked hot spicy meals on cold, sleety days, too. They could go to the Iron Maiden, that funky new Ukranian restaurant on Charles, or maybe try for some Szechuan, or even order in some Mexican.

A rumble of thunder pulled Julia out of her reverie. She wouldn't be going anywhere with Dora this evening. She wouldn't be renting a movie or buying herself a new book. She probably wouldn't even have heat.

What am I doing here, she thought, *in a place where the only fast food is deer?*

The irony of it was that Dora and everyone else thought she was in Florida. Herbert Davis had instructed her to call the office and ask for unpaid compassionate leave to tend a sick grandfather in St.

Petersburg. At irregular but frequent intervals, postcards signed by her were mailed from Florida to her office colleagues and to a list of friends Davis had told Julia to draw up. Probably Jean and Dora were envying her right now, getting to spend time down in Florida, basking in the sunshine, doing well by doing good.

The unfairness of it ate like acid into Julia's soul. Her mind raced back to that terrible, terrible day, two months earlier.

It had been hot then. A typical muggy Boston August day. In slow motion, like a nightmare, she saw once more the scene she could never forget: the scrawny stranger on his knees, the sweat of fear dripping on the oil-stained pavement, the large, cruel-faced man pointing a gun at him, finger slowly tightening on the trigger. Then. . . .

Another rumble of thunder caused the lights to flicker in the shadowed room.

Heavy footsteps sounded in the corridor outside the classroom, loud in the silence of the school. Someone was striding quickly, then stopping, then walking quickly again, as if—her heart started racing—as if looking for something, or *someone*.

Don't be silly, she told herself, but her heart continued its wild thumping. She pushed papers into her briefcase with shaking hands, cursing as one sheet slipped to the floor. She could hear herself panting and made a conscious effort to slow her breathing. The footsteps stopped, then started again. Each teacher had his or her name taped to the door. If someone was looking for Sally Andersen—

Stop, start.

She grabbed her coat, trying to calm her trembling. It was probably the janitor, Jim—*except that Jim was an old man and shuffled;* or one of the teachers— *except that all the other teachers had gone home.*

The footsteps stopped at her door and her gaze froze on the glass pane that covered the upper half of the door. She had to see who was out there, reassure herself that it was just one of the harmless citizens of Simpson and not—

A face pressed against the window. A man. He reached inside his jacket and started to pull something from his pocket.

And then the lights went out.

Julia whimpered and tried to think despite the icy fear that gripped her. *What could she use as a weapon?* There was nothing in her purse but a pocket diary, keys and makeup. The students' desks were too heavy to lift, and the chairs were of lightweight plastic. Her hand brushed something hard and round. Mr. Big!

Panting wildly, she hoisted the enormous pumpkin in her arms and stood at the side of the door, ready to smash the intruder over the head. Her body tensed, going into fight-and-flight mode.

The doorknob rattled.

Julia closed her eyes and saw again the face that had been revealed in the bright neon lights of the corridor.

Overlong, straight black hair, framing a series of slabs angling harshly together to form cheeks and chin, a straight slash of a mouth, black eyes.

An unfamiliar face, an unforgettable face—a killer's face.

Two

Richard Cooper felt like killing someone, prefer-ably his foreman and best friend, Bernaldo Martinez. Or, failing that, Bernie's cheating wife, Carmelita.

They should be the ones here, ready to talk to little Rafael's teacher, not him. He'd rather walk across hot coals than do this. He hadn't the faintest idea what he could possibly say to Rafael's teacher. He only knew that Bernie was in no condition to talk to any-one right now.

Cooper reached into his jacket to touch the notes the teacher, a Miss Sally Andersen, had sent home with the little boy. He knew them all by heart, having reread them a dozen times since coming home after a business trip to Boise and finding Bernie passed out, clutching an empty bottle of cheap bourbon in one fist and one of the notes in the other.

Bernie was going to owe him, big time. Playing nursemaid and facing grade school teachers were not high on Cooper's list of favorite pastimes.

Cooper stood outside the door of the schoolroom. The little plaque outside the door confirmed that this was Miss Andersen's classroom. He pressed his face against the glass pane of the door, hoping the room would be empty, but the lights in the corridor were so bright all he could see was his own face reflected back at him. He looked as annoyed as he felt.

He turned the doorknob, and then a thousand tons of brick fell on his head.

"Wha—?" Cooper found himself against the classroom wall, legs splayed out. He put a hand to his head and it came away wet. *Pumpkin?* He stared for a moment at his hand, covered with pumpkin pulp and seeds. *He'd been brained with a pumpkin?*

"Don't move," a high voice warned him. A small, slender woman faced him, panting and terrified.

He froze. She held a small spray can aimed at him. It was a replica of a breath freshener he had in his bathroom. "This is mace," she gasped. "If you make a move, just one move, I'll spray you."

He stayed put.

Footsteps sounded in the corridor. Keeping wide eyes on him, the woman edged toward the door.

"Jim!" she yelled. "Call the sheriff! Tell him I've got a dangerous criminal here. Tell him to get over here *now!*" Julia shifted her gaze slightly and saw Jim drop his mop and hustle out the door. Her eyes flickered back to the man sitting against the wall.

Even sitting down, he was terrifying. Smashing him with Mr. Big hadn't knocked him out. Long, lean, dressed in a black turtleneck sweater, a black bomber jacket and jeans, he looked every inch a killer. Her hand trembled. Thank God she had thought of the little spray can of breath freshener in her purse.

"Don't move," Julia said again, breathlessly. She was so frightened she had trouble breathing. The terror of the past two months came rushing back tenfold, all wrapped up in one long, lean package.

Obsidian-black eyes glittered at her, and she knew that he was calculating his next move. How long could she hope to keep him at bay?

She was terrified, Cooper realized.

She should have been a redhead. Though her hair was a rather dull shade of brown, she had the pale skin and deep turquoise eyes of a redhead and she reminded him of a fox cub he had once come across, its paw caught in a trap. The cub was mortally wounded and he wanted only to free it from the trap, but the cub had hissed and growled and tried to bite him with its baby milk teeth.

The door to the school opened and running footsteps sounded in the corridor. The classroom door was yanked open and Chuck Pedersen filled the doorway, a pistol in his hand.

He skidded to a stop, taking in Cooper sprawled on the floor and a young woman crouching in a policeman's shooting stance, holding a can of breath freshener.

"Officer." Her voice came out in a squeak. She coughed to clear her tight throat and began again. "Officer, arrest that man! He's a dangerous criminal."

Sheriff Pedersen holstered his pistol and leaned against the doorframe, drinking in the sight of Cooper on his backside against a wall with obvious pleasure. "Hey, Coop."

"Chuck."

Julia locked her knees because she could feel that they were about to give way. She looked at the sheriff. "You know this man?"

Sheriff Pedersen shifted his considerable weight and transferred his chewing gum from one cheek to the other. "Know?" he asked philosophically. "What does it mean to 'know' someone? You can spend years with a man and never really understand—"

"Chuck," the man on the floor said, his low voice a growl.

Pedersen shrugged. "Yeah," he said, turning to Julia. "I know Richard Cooper. Known him all his life. Knew his dad. Hell, even knew his grandpappy."

"Oh, no." Julia couldn't get her insides to stop. They felt as if they were racing at a thousand miles an hour. Adrenaline was still pumping through her bloodstream and she couldn't connect her thoughts.

She had fully expected to die as she bravely defended herself against a vicious contract killer, but she had only knocked out a good citizen of Simpson.

The man was still sitting on the floor, glaring up at her. Julia tried to think of something reasonable to say. How on earth could she apologize? *Excuse me for having attacked you, but I thought that you were a hired killer and things kind of got out of hand,* sounded a little lame.

Still, it hadn't been such a wild leap of the imagination. He certainly looked dangerous. There wasn't a thing about him that was soft or gentle. He was lean, broad-shouldered, and his features were attractively rugged. He was also dark in coloring, which was why she'd assumed he wasn't from Simpson.

After about a week in the town, Julia realized why Herbert Davis had given her the assumed name of Sally Andersen. It seemed as if everyone in Simpson was a Jensen, a Jorgensen or a Pedersen. She was sure that sometime in the last century, a bedraggled group of Scandinavian settlers aiming for the Pacific Ocean had just given up and decided to stay put by the time they reached western Idaho. Everyone in Simpson seemed to share the same genes for pale complexions and pale blond hair.

Not the man she'd had a little round of assault and battery with, though. Nothing pale and blond about *him*.

He had jet-black hair and jet-black eyes, matching his jet-black bomber jacket and the black stubble covering his cheeks. The only light-colored thing about him was the pumpkin pulp.

Julia swallowed around the lump of guilt in her throat. She surreptitiously slipped the breath freshener back in her purse. "Er—how do you do? My name's Ju—Sally Andersen." She tried to keep the waver out of her voice, but it wasn't easy.

"Richard Cooper," he said and stood up in one lithe movement.

"Most people call him Coop," the sheriff offered.

Julia wondered what her mother, a stickler for correctness, would have thought about the etiquette of the situation. Was it permissible to use a nickname for someone you'd done your best to knock unconscious? Probably not.

"Mr. Cooper."

"Miss Andersen." She had a momentary pang of doubt, because his voice sounded like a killer's voice, deep, low and raspy. She took another look at him.

He still looked dangerous.

"You're *sure* you know this man, Sheriff?"

"Yes, ma'am." Sheriff Pedersen grinned. "Raises horses on a big spread between here and Rupert. All kinds of horses, Arabian, Appaloosa, quarter—"

"I, um, I guess I owe you an apology, Mr. Cooper."

Julia tried to think of something logical to say. "I—I mistook you for someone else."

An embarrassing silence fell over the room.

"Can't believe you let someone get the drop on you, Coop." The sheriff chuckled. " 'Specially a girl."

"Woman," Julia murmured.

"What? Oh, yeah, can't call girls 'girls' anymore." The sheriff shook his head in sorrow. He looked Julia up and down and cackled at Cooper. "I'll bet you have ten inches and seventy pounds on her, Coop. You must be getting soft." He turned to Julia. "Coop used to be a SEAL, you know."

A seal?

Julia absorbed this information as she looked at Richard Cooper. Splayed on the floor, he had looked somewhat dangerous. On his feet, he was terrifying. She observed him carefully, paying particular attention to his alarmingly large hands, and turned to the sheriff.

"That may be," she said politely. "But his flippers are gone now."

The sheriff stared at her for a moment, and wheezed heavily once, then twice. It was only when he bent double, shoulders shaking, that Julia realized he was laughing.

It was the last straw. The whole, miserable day came crashing in on her. Herbert Davis and his less than reassuring news that someone might have come close to discovering where she was, the terror when she thought one of Santana's killers had found her, her heroic last stand, the overwhelming relief when she'd discovered that she might live, after all.

Then the sheriff running to her rescue, only he hadn't rescued her at all. Actually, he could probably have her arrested for—for what? Assault with a deadly vegetable?

"If you don't *mind,* Sheriff," she said coldly.

Chuck Pedersen wheezed once more and wiped his eyes. "Flippers," he said and wheezed again. He shook his head. "No, Miss—"

Templeton, she thought. "Andersen," she said.

"Andersen, that's right. Sorry. You just moved here a few months ago, right?"

"That's correct."

"So you don't know everyone in the area yet. But old Coop, here, he used to be a Navy SEAL. Stands for Sea Air and Land commandos. Crack troops. Coop did damned well, too, got hisself a medal, he did. Then his daddy died and he came back to run the Cooper spread."

Julia closed her eyes for a moment. This was worse than she'd thought. It wasn't bad enough that she'd assaulted one of the good citizens of Simpson. She'd clobbered a *war hero.* She opened her eyes and stole a look at him again.

Gathering the few tattered shreds of her dignity, she held out her hand to Richard Cooper.

She stared straight into his black, expressionless eyes and shivered. "Please accept my apologies, Mr. Cooper."

After a moment, Cooper took her hand. His was hard and callused and Julia held his hand and he held her eyes. Julia stared, then slipped her hand from his grasp and turned away, feeling as if she'd just escaped a force-field. He made a sound, and she decided to take it as acceptance of her apology, remembering that seals didn't talk.

They just grunted.

* * *

She's still scared, Cooper thought. Her hand had trembled in his. It had been soft and small and icy cold and he was surprised at the sudden urge he'd had to keep holding it, just to warm it up. He'd resisted, because she still looked frightened of him. It was hard to forget the look of sheer terror on her face. The last time he'd seen anyone look like that had been under gunfire. She was hiding it well now, with a polite expression on her pretty face. But her hand had trembled.

Julia turned to the sheriff and tried to smile. "I guess I owe you my apologies as well, Sheriff."

"Call me Chuck." The sheriff grinned. "We don't stand much on ceremony around here."

"Chuck, then. I'm really sorry I caused all this commotion."

He rocked back on his heels. "Well, I won't say anytime, because you gave me a fright there, Miss Andersen—"

"Sally," Julia said, hating the name.

"Sally. As I was saying, I thought I'd caught myself a criminal. Mostly what I do is break up a few fights on Saturday night and arrest speeders. Not many of those, either."

"No, I imagine not," Julia murmured. "Simpson seems like such a nice little town." After all she'd been through that afternoon, what was a little lie? All right, a big lie. "Friendly and quiet."

The sheriff beamed. "That it is. Glad you like it here. We're always happy to welcome newcomers to Simpson. We need new blood. The youngsters keep leaving us, right after high school. I keep telling 'em it's a nasty world out there, but nobody listens. Can't imagine what they think they're gonna find out there."

Oh, I don't know, Julia thought. *Bookshops, cinema, theater, art galleries. Human beings.* Then, because she'd always been told her face was an open book, she smiled and tried to think of something else. "You know what kids are like. I guess they feel they have to go and find out for themselves."

Out of politeness Julia turned to the man she'd brained. "Isn't that right, Mr. Cooper?"

Cooper started. He'd been thinking how easy this Sally Andersen was finding it to talk to Chuck even after five minutes' acquaintance. He'd found it enormously difficult to tell Chuck how sorry he'd been when Carly, Chuck's wife, had passed away. And Chuck had just stood around morosely, patting him awkwardly on the back when his own wife, Melissa, had left. Looked like pretty grade school teachers didn't have the kind of problems men did. Particularly not pretty schoolteachers with red, no—he checked again while she wasn't looking—brown hair.

It ought to be red. She had a redhead's complexion.

There was a sudden silence, and Chuck and the teacher were both looking at him in expectation. The echo of Miss Andersen's question hovered in the air.

"Er, that's right." It must have been an appropriate response, because the teacher gathered her things and slipped out the door and Chuck patted him on the back and followed her and he was left alone in the school, except for Jim, out swabbing the corridor.

Cooper moved toward the door and heard something crackle. The notes. The notes Sally Andersen had written. He'd come here to talk about Rafael.

Damn. He'd forgotten all about it.

A million dollars.

The professional stared at the computer screen. It looked like Dominic Santana was willing to pay a million dollars to get rid of Julia Templeton. The chick had been in the wrong place at the wrong time and—bad luck for her—had captured the entire hit on film. When Santana finally came to trial, Julia Templeton was going to be Witness Numero Uno.

Julia Templeton had disappeared immediately after the hit. A phone call to a talkative secretary at Warwick Publishing had elicited the information that she was in Florida, tending a sick grandfather, but the pro knew better. Julia Templeton had without a doubt gone straight into the Witness Protection Program.

Three

It was a short walk from the school to Julia's home.

It was a short walk to anywhere in Simpson. She didn't really need the clunky lime-green Fairlane Herbert Davis had made available.

She missed her classy Fiat.

She missed her classy life.

She walked up the rickety steps of her wooden porch which was badly in need of repair and inserted the key. She stopped when she heard a scrabbling sound and her heart beat faster. *Was there someone on her porch, waiting for her?*

She spied a dusty brown beast at the edge of the porch and sagged in relief. Just a stray dog. The dog was huddled in the corner of the porch. Julia approached him gingerly. She didn't know anything about dogs.

"Nice doggy," she said unconvincingly as she approached the matted heap of fur. She couldn't even tell which end was head and which end was tail. The dog took care of her uncertainty by lifting a pointed, stained muzzle and thumping the other end on the floorboards.

She squatted to look at him in the uncertain light from the streetlamp. The dog's tail thumped weakly on the boards as Julia reached out to pat it. She felt something wet and snatched her hand back, then realized that the dog was trying to lick her hand. The dog lifted its muzzle. Julia could swear that it was looking straight into her soul. The mutt looked lost and lonely.

"You, too, huh?" she murmured and, with a sigh, bent to gather the dog in her arms. She dropped him when he whined loudly. "What's the matter? Are you hurt?" She gently ran her hands over the dull coat, trying not to think about ticks and fleas and stopped when she felt the right foreleg.

"Broken, huh?" she asked the dog. "Or maybe sprained. I don't know. I hope Simpson has a vet." She pursed her lips and looked at the dog sternly. "You can come in tonight because it's cold and you're hurt, but just for the night and then you're out. Is that clear?"

His tail swished again and he licked her hand.

"Okay, just as long as we understand each other." Julia lifted the surprisingly heavy dog in her arms, staggering a little. "And no home-cooked meals either. You'll get some bread and milk and that's it." The dog whined again as they crossed the threshold. Julia sighed. "Well, maybe if you're really good, you can have my leftover tuna casserole."

She put some old towels on the floor in the corner of the little living room and stepped back. He was a big dog, though he looked half-starved. His ribs were sticking out so clearly through his dull, matted coat that she could count each one of them.

Julia went into the kitchen, poured milk into a bowl and put the remains of her tuna casserole on a plate. The dog gulped the food down and slurped up the milk. He gazed at her through half-closed eyes.

"Hard times, huh, big fellow?" Julia asked softly. The dog yawned, showing a mouthful of yellow teeth, put its nose on its forepaws and went out like a light. Julia envied him. She hadn't had a decent night's sleep in two months. It would take more than a blanket and some leftover tuna casserole to repair her shattered life.

Julia shivered. Speaking of repairs . . .

Reluctantly, she walked into the pantry—actually a little cubbyhole just off the kitchen—where some joker with a misguided sense of humor had installed something that looked sort of like a gigantic water heater crossed with a boiler. But the only thing the big tank did was take the edge off the chill and provide, with an inordinate amount of moaning and groaning, a reluctant trickle of tepid water.

Or had done, until this morning, when her shower had been icy cold and she had noticed a water stain on the wall. The stain had spread, and now there was water on the floor and an alarming gurgling sound.

Her front doorbell rang. With a last, baffled look at the criss-crossing tangle of tubes and piping, she walked to the door and yanked it open.

Windblown gusts of sleet streaked diagonally across the cone of light from the streetlamp. Julia shivered. The temperature had dropped another ten degrees.

Richard Cooper stood in her doorway, tall, dressed in black, with a grim expression on his face. She stared at him for a long moment, then gathered her courage in both hands. "Are you going to press charges?" she asked, lifting her chin.

He blinked. Something, some unreadable expression crossed his face. "No, I'm not."

"Oh." Some of the tension deserted her. "That's good."

"I came because—" Cooper started.

There was a loud crash and the sound of water splashing on the floor.

"Oh, no!" Julia groaned and ran to the pantry. Water was seeping from the wall, spreading out from where the water stain had been. Then she heard something pop and water cascaded out in an arc, taking great chunks of plaster with it.

"Where's the main distribution pipe valve?"

Julia turned at the sound of the harsh voice behind her. She stared helplessly at Richard Cooper. He felt his way around the watery mess until he found something and wrenched his wrist to the right. Like magic, the water stopped spouting.

Then he knelt and started pulling out chunks of her wall. He stuck both hands into the innards of her house, eventually ending up on his side, his head stuck into the wall. Julia heard him grunt, then he pulled his head out.

"Lug," he said. Right to her face.

Julia stiffened. She hadn't the faintest idea what lug meant, but surely it wasn't very complimentary.

"I beg your pardon," she said huffily.

A faint smile crossed his austere features. "I need a lug wrench to fix the pipe." He pulled some keys from his jeans pocket. "These are the keys to the pickup. Toolbox's on the front seat."

Julia stared down into his face, taking in the hard, dark features and dark eyes glittering at her. She opened her mouth to say something, then closed it again and walked out to her little front garden. Sure enough, a battered pickup was parked outside. It was black.

Figured.

Through the passenger window Julia could see a steel toolbox, the kind handymen had. The third key she tried opened the pickup door, and she pulled out the toolbox. It weighed a ton. Puffing, she carried it inside and shook off the mixture of rain and ice.

"Here."

Cooper rifled through what looked like a senseless jumble of tools and picked up a wicked-looking implement.

"This." When Julia looked at him in bafflement, Cooper sighed. "This is a lug wrench."

"Oh," Julia said and smiled.

Cooper would have been floored by the charm of that smile had he not already been stretched out on the floor. It transformed her face. He'd seen her terrified and annoyed and baffled and angry—and now delighted—in the space of half an hour. Each emotion had been so clearly visible it could have been written on her forehead. His ex-wife Melissa had called him stone-faced so often he'd begun to believe he couldn't show an emotion if he tried.

Sally Andersen's smile had faded now and Cooper realized that he'd been staring at her. He tried a smile himself and felt unused cheek muscles crack. He couldn't hold the smile for much longer, so he bent back to the task of putting her plumbing in order.

While he worked in silence, Julia mopped up the mess. She had to step more than once around Richard Cooper's long legs, which seemed to stretch out forever. *Nice legs,* she thought distractedly, then was ashamed of herself for ogling the legs of a man who was helping her. They were long, lean and muscular, the strong thigh muscles outlined by his tight jeans. The jeans were almost white in places. Not the chic, prestressed kind, but the kind that got worn in the right places from working hard in them for a long time. He had on cowboy boots, also well worn. The heels needed repairing. Crazily, Julia was reassured by the faded jeans and dusty, scratched boots. In every film she'd ever seen, hired killers were dapper and wouldn't be caught dead in faded clothes and down-at-the-heel boots.

Richard Cooper seemed like a perfectly nice man. Just a little communication-challenged.

Half an hour later, Cooper straightened and wiped his hands on a cloth. He held his hands up. "May I wash my hands?"

"Of course." The house was already beginning to heat up and Julia felt an enormous surge of gratitude toward him. Okay, so he didn't talk much, but who needed a man who could talk when he could repair plumbing? "The bathroom is the second door to the right. The towels are clean."

She'd make him a cup of tea, or maybe cowboys preferred coffee. She started for the kitchen and heard a knock on the door.

Julia opened the door and her worst nightmare came out of the swirling darkness.

A pistol. Aimed straight at her head.

Four

Julia screamed and her heart started to pound its way out of her chest.

"Trick or treat." The childish voice came from somewhere around her knees and she froze. These weren't killers, just schoolkids wanting a treat.

It was too much.

The front door closed. Dimly, as if coming from a hundred miles away, Julia heard a deep male voice and the excited squeals of children from the porch. Then, a moment later, the front door opened again, letting in an arctic swirl of wind.

Terror, loneliness, despair all seemed to jostle sharply, painfully inside Julia's chest, as if there were knives in there fighting their way out, slicing her heart into shreds. She drew in a long, sobbing breath as another tear squeezed out from behind her closed lids. Rough tremors shook her. In the instant before her knees gave way, she felt herself half-lifted and turned against a solid chest.

To Julia's intense horror, short, stuttering sobs racked through her. She felt a large hand covering the back of her head and she let herself go limp. It felt like a lifetime since she had been held and comforted by another human being. Since the death of her parents, in fact. And now Julia found herself weeping out her fear and anger and loneliness in great, uncontrollable gasping sobs which she couldn't have held back had her life depended on it.

Some part of her knew that she was weeping her heart out all over Richard Cooper's black sweater and that she was going to be deeply ashamed.

In a few minutes.

But right now there was something immensely comforting in the still, broad figure who held her close enough to soothe, yet loosely enough so that she could move away any time she wanted.

The tears dried up, but the hot hard tangle of pain in her chest still hurt.

Cooper loosened his grip and walked away, coming back immediately.

"Here." He curled Julia's hand around a glass half full of liquid. Gratefully, she gulped it down then yelped as it burned its way to her stomach.

"What was that?" she gasped, looking up at him. Her eyes filled again with tears, but a better variety of tears. "Liquid fire?"

"Whisky," Cooper said and took the glass from her numb hand. All of her was numb, except the parts that were hot.

"Where did you get that?" Julia gave one last cough then put a hand to her stomach, where a warm ball had settled.

"I had it."

"In your *toolbox?*" Julia blinked at Cooper in amazement.

"No." Cooper's mouth twitched, which she supposed was cowboy body language for amusement. "In the pickup. For emergencies."

For a second, Julia wanted to ask what kind of emergency, but one look at that angular, shuttered face and she bit her tongue. Well, of course. In the movies, cowboys were always getting shot, then they poured whisky over the wound. Just before digging the bullet out with a hunting knife by the light of a campfire.

The whisky was going to her head. Or the adrenaline had deserted her body in a rush. Whatever the cause, Julia suddenly felt weak. Completely drained, she slumped onto the sofa, while Cooper sat down on the matching armchair.

Silence fell over the room. "I can't talk about it," Julia blurted out when the silence began to be embarrassing. She lifted her chin belligerently.

Cooper nodded his head once, gravely, as if that were the most reasonable statement he'd ever heard and Julia slumped in relief. At least he wouldn't start pumping her for information on her bizarre behavior.

She jumped when something cold and wet poked at her hand.

"Oh!" Julia bent over the arm of the chair and looked down into soulful brown eyes. It was crazy, probably induced by stress and alcohol, but she had the feeling that the stray she'd taken in understood everything she was going through. The dog gazed at her adoringly, then licked her hand.

"Do you repair animals as well as plumbing, Mr., um, Cooper?"

"Just Cooper'll do, ma'am."

He rose easily from the armchair, which was no

mean feat. Julia knew the springs on that armchair were broken, and she had struggled more than once to get out of it. But Cooper rose out of it just as smoothly as if the chair had lifted itself up to tip him out, which meant that he had fantastic abdominals. Actually, Julia thought abstractedly, as Cooper bent over the dog, he had fantastic everything.

He moved with an incredibly lithe, athletic grace. Long, lean muscles showed through the black sweater. His hands, now moving gently over the dog, were large, long-fingered and graceful. When he hunkered down to murmur softly to the animal, Julia noticed again how strong his thigh muscles were. She had never really thought about male thigh muscles before. Probably because she'd never seen such fine ones before.

Cooper looked up at her and Julia found herself blushing furiously, the blood pumping hard and hot into her face. *Just how much whisky had there been in that glass?* she thought in a panic, and rushed in to cover her embarrassment.

"He's not really mine, you know. I just found him on my front porch this evening when I came home after—" *After braining you with a pumpkin,* she didn't say.

Julia wondered if she looked as confused as she felt.

Cooper gave no notice. Those large, gorgeous male hands were running over the dog's body and stopped at the right foreleg.

"I noticed that, too. Is it broken?" Julia peered over the couch.

"No. Sprained. And someone's been abusing him." Cooper gave a few more reassuring sounds

which had even Julia lulled, then looked up again.
"This dog have a name?"

"No. I told you he just showed up this evening."

"Needs a name." Cooper gently ruffled the matted
fur between the dog's ears.

"Ah—" The mangy, yellow-haired dog was as far
away from her sleek Siamese cat, Federico, as it was
possible to be. Still, the mutt had four legs and a
head, just like Federico. Close enough. "Fred. I want
to call him Fred."

"Fred, it is." Cooper let the dog sniff his fingers
once again. "He'll be all right in a few days if he
keeps his weight off that paw. A few good meals and
a warm place to sleep is all he needs." Cooper picked
a burr from the dog's coat, then stood up suddenly.
Julia found herself craning her neck to look up at
him.

"Are you going?" She had a sudden, unexplained
panicky feeling.

"No." He looked down at her a moment, expressionless, and she found herself wishing she could
read what he was thinking.

He opened the door and disappeared. It was night
now, and Julia caught a glimpse of darkness and driving sleet in the light from the streetlamp. Before she
had time to feel the cold from the door he was back,
holding a first aid kit.

"Does that come from the magic pickup, too?"

Again, she had a fleeting impression of a smile.
"That's right."

Cooper knelt down to Fred and started murmuring
again, soothing, senseless noises. Julia was astonished
to see that the dog made no protest, even when Cooper examined his forepaw carefully and wrapped an

elastic bandage around it. There was a deep scratch on the dog's right haunch, and though Fred whined when Cooper examined it, he didn't move. Cooper cleaned the wound, but didn't bandage it.

Julia leaned over the arm of the sofa and watched Cooper with interest. He worked quickly, quietly and competently.

"What do you suppose happened to him?"

Cooper sat back on his heels, stretching the jeans. Julia carefully kept her eyes on his face. This sudden fascination with his thigh muscles had to be the result of stress and whisky.

Cooper's face was as hard as the rest of him.

"Car accident most likely," he said after a long moment, during which Julia wondered in sudden panic whether he was a mind reader. If he were, she'd die of embarrassment. "Either hit by a car or thrown out of one."

Julia sharply sucked in her breath, outraged. "Thrown out! You mean someone would deliberately throw an animal out of a moving car?"

"Uh-huh. Happens all the time. Someone thought they wanted a pet, then changed their mind. Fred is definitely someone's dog, though. Or was. Got good clean lines, probably make a good hunter." Cooper's large hand brushed the top of Fred's head, thumb idly scratching behind his ears. Fred's bushy tail thumped heavily.

"If you say so." Julia looked doubtfully at Fred. "I'm not a dog person myself and I really have no intention of keeping him. I just felt sorry for him tonight."

Cooper stood up and stuck his hands in his jeans

pockets. "You might want to keep him for a while. Be company when you—" He stopped suddenly.

"When I fall apart?" Julia asked dryly. "I assure you, Mr. Cooper, I'm not in the habit of falling to pieces every evening."

"Didn't think you were, ma'am." He shifted his weight from one dusty boot to another, graceful even when embarrassed. "And the name's Cooper."

Julia tilted her head as she examined him. "Doesn't anyone call you by your first name? What is it? Richard?"

"Yup. But most everyone calls me Coop."

"Even when you were a child? What did your mother call you?"

"Don't know. She died when I was three. Hardly remember her."

"What did they call you at school?"

"Coop."

"And your wife?"

"Mostly she called me an SOB, ma'am." His black eyes bored into hers. " 'Specially just before she left me."

Well, that was a conversation stopper, Julia thought, surprised by his bluntness.

"Oh. I, ah . . . sorry. I didn't mean to pry, it's just that . . ." Julia wound down with an embarrassed shrug, then watched curiously as Cooper pulled a note out of his shirt pocket and handed it to her.

Surprised, she unfolded it, only to find that it was one of the notes she had written and addressed to Rafael's parents. It didn't matter which note it was, they all said more or less the same thing. *Rafael is having serious problems at school, and I would appreciate a chance to talk it over with you.*

She looked at the tall, silent man before her, then back at the note. "I don't really see—" Then, suddenly, she did.

Obviously, Richard Cooper was little Rafael's father. Julia's fertile imagination filled in the blanks. Cooper's wife—the one who called him an SOB—must have recently left him, which must be why little Rafael was having so many problems.

No, that didn't work.

Rafael's last name was Martinez, not Cooper, so she couldn't have been his wife. But he *had* said his *wife* had left him, so maybe Rafael was Cooper's wife's child from a first marriage, his ex-wife's child—it was hard to work it all out in her mind while those opaque black eyes were steadily watching her.

"Look, I apologize for interfering, but Rafael really is having problems coping at school. Why just today, he cried because Missy—"

"Tomorrow," Cooper interrupted. "Could you come out?"

She was starting to be able to decipher his laconic cowboy code. Translated into normal conversation, Cooper was asking her if she would be willing to come out to the ranch tomorrow and talk over Rafael's problems.

"Yes, of course," she said. "Where's your house, er, ranch?"

"Drive five miles west out the old McMurphy Road toward the interstate, turn right at the intersection, then drive northeast for two miles, take the south fork, drive four hundred yards . . ."

Cooper watched her bright, pretty face as she listened to him without changing expression. He swallowed a sigh.

"I'm coming into town tomorrow morning," he lied. "Could you be at the diner around ten?"

"The diner," Julia said, enormously relieved. "Ten o'clock tomorrow." For a minute there, she thought she'd have to go out all by herself. Five miles west . . . south fork . . . four hundred yards. He might as well have been speaking Greek. "I'll be there."

"Fine." He dipped his head gravely. "Thank you."

"Don't mention it." Julia said softly. "It's the least I can do after . . ." she waved a hand awkwardly, fighting the urge to pantomime dropping a big pumpkin on Cooper's head.

Cooper was in the open doorway now. It was still sleeting and the temperature had dropped precipitously. His breath created a wreath around his head, making him look slightly unreal. Those strong, unhandsome, craggy features seemed chiseled from stone, as if he were a statue in the mist instead of a human being in the cold. Only his eyes glittered. Julia was no longer frightened of him, however forbidding he looked. He seemed so remote, so untouchable. Yet he'd shown her, and Fred, nothing but kindness. It was hard to square that kindness with a man who could make his little son so miserable.

They were so close she was getting a crick in her neck looking up at him. Fred kept swinging his head back and forth to look at his new friends.

"Rafael," she said breathlessly. She found it impossible to tear her eyes from Cooper's face. "He's such a nice little boy. I'm sure that with a little bit of help, things will straighten themselves out."

Cooper knew he was staring and wondered if she found him as strange as everyone else did lately. But he couldn't turn away.

It wasn't just that she was a very pretty young woman, though attractive women certainly didn't grow on trees in Simpson. Rather, it was something about the quality of her skin, pale and so luminous it seemed to glow as if there were a light within. Or maybe it was her clear turquoise eyes, the color of the sky over his ranch on a hot summer day. Whatever it was, he couldn't tear his eyes away.

He had to go. He was standing blocking her doorway and precious heat was dissipating into the frigid night. Wisps of steamy warm air curled around his legs. He told his feet to move, but it took a few seconds for his boots to register the message. He turned and walked across the rickety porch. The second step down had a loose plank and he made a mental note to fix it for her. It was the least he could do, if she was willing to help Rafael.

A sudden thought made him stop and turn around. She was still standing in the doorway. "Miss Andersen—"

"Sally," she said. Her slender form was backlit and he couldn't see her face.

"Okay, Sally. Rafael is . . ." Cooper hesitated.

"Yes, Cooper?" Her voice sounded soft in the darkness. "Rafael is what?"

"He's not my boy," Cooper said, then turned on his heel, climbed up into his pickup truck and drove away into the black, sleety night.

Five

Julia stopped in the middle of the empty street and huddled in on herself, rubbing her arms. The day was much chillier than she had anticipated, and her light jacket was no match for the icy wind. She felt cold and lost. *What am I doing here?* she thought suddenly. She felt almost paralyzed with depression and anxiety. What *was* she doing?

Escaping a killer, that was what.

Julia shivered again, then almost jumped when something heavy and warm was dropped around her shoulders. It was Cooper's black leather jacket, and it hung almost to her knees. She put down her briefcase and slipped her arms into the sleeves, savoring the warmth for a moment. She looked up. "Thanks." She tried to smile but her teeth were chattering. "I didn't think it would be this cold. But what about you?" She awkwardly waved the heavy leather sleeve at him. Only her fingertips showed.

"I don't mind the cold," Cooper said. He bent to pick up her briefcase, cupped her elbow, and helped her up into his black Blazer.

Julia stared out the window as he circled the vehicle. He didn't talk much, but he sure had a knack for making her feel cared for.

* * *

"Er, how's Rafael?" Julia asked, more to hear the sound of a human being's voice than to hear the answer.

"Fine," Cooper replied. It was his third word in twenty minutes. The other two had been "yes," and "no," in answer to direct questions. Julia gave up and looked at the scenery. It was either that or look at Cooper, and she found to her astonishment that looking at him was very disturbing, so she tried to keep her eyes away.

He was a superb driver.

Julia really admired good driving, mainly because she was such a lousy driver herself. But Cooper was concentrated and relaxed, playing the gearshift like a musical instrument.

Maybe he wasn't much of a talker, but he was a real ace behind the wheel.

Julia didn't usually notice whether a man was a good driver, or whether he had strong hands or long legs. Yet she was stirringly aware of the tall, dark, *silent*—though certainly not handsome—man sitting next to her and, for the life of her, she couldn't figure out why. Certainly not for his brilliant conversation, which was what usually attracted her to a man. Up until now, she would have sworn that all her sexual responses were in her head. She'd get interested when a man shared her taste in literature, or was a witty conversationalist, or he made her laugh.

She was usually not attracted to a man because his large, strong hands, with a light dusting of black hairs on the back, rested with easy, elegant competence on the wheel of a car, or because the muscles in his forearm did a fascinating dance every time he shifted gears, or because when he popped the clutch, lean muscles played under the black slacks from his knees to his groin. Julia whipped her head around and stared blindly out the window.

Something was definitely wrong with her. Stress, or the silence, was driving her crazy. She wasn't used to silence. Maybe if she talked to him, this weird spell she was under would be broken.

"Is it far?"

Cooper's gaze flicked briefly over to her. "Actually, we're here."

Julia stared. "We are?" She took a good look around. She couldn't see anything but what had been there for the past half hour: trees, grass, trees, grass and more trees.

"We've been on Double C land for over ten minutes now," Cooper said. Sure enough, now that he mentioned it, she could see fences neatly laid out, running parallel to the road and in the far distance, toward a range of hills. They turned into a well-kept driveway.

There was so much to see, and all of it foreign to her, that it took Julia a few moments to sort out her impressions. The fencing was white now and enclosed large, freshly painted buildings and circular areas full of sand. Ten or twelve men were working, some raking the grounds, several leading horses by what looked like a single long rein, a few on horseback. The impression was of a bustling, prosperous business.

Cooper slowed the Blazer, and they drove by what Julia at first took for a geological formation. Then she looked again. No geological formation she knew of was rectangular and made of wood. "What's that?"

she breathed and waved her hand at the vast old house they were driving by.

"The house." Cooper finally turned a corner and brought the Blazer to a halt in a carport of more modern design.

"Who built it?" She tore her eyes away from the mansion and looked quizzically at Cooper.

"My great-grandfather." He circled the vehicle and came to open Julia's door, cupping her elbow until she was safely on the cement floor of the carport.

Julia smiled up at him and Cooper forgot to let go of her elbow. "Looks like he had to fell a forest to build this thing."

Cooper was distracted by her smile and didn't answer for a long moment. Then he noticed that his hand was still holding her elbow and he reluctantly dropped it. It was harder to do than he would have thought.

"My great-grandfather believed in elbow room."

"No kidding. You can probably see this from outer space." Julia stepped out from under the carport roof and looked around. She had to move her head to take all the house in, since close up it was bigger than her field of vision. "How many Coopers actually live here?"

"Just me," Cooper said, hoping she liked the old place.

Those stunning turquoise eyes stopped looking at the enormous house and fixed on him. They were not only beautiful but also disturbingly intelligent. She stared at him, that blue gaze direct and unblinking. "Just you?"

Cooper stifled a sigh. "Yeah."

"Not even an odd cousin or two lost somewhere in the house?"

"Nope." Cooper fought the urge to fidget. "My great-grandfather had one child and my grandfather had one child and my father—"

"Wait," Julia said. "Let me guess." Cooper watched, fascinated, as the dimple peeped then disappeared. "One child, a son. You."

"Bingo." Cooper was uncomfortable and he didn't want any more questions. What he wanted was to hold her arm again. "That first step is a bit steep," he lied as he took her arm and steered her over to the stairs that led up into the kitchen. "You want to watch it."

Julia barely had time to take in everything, because Cooper was holding her arm in an iron grip, and he seemed to want to march her around the house, through long, dark, musty corridors where she caught glimpses of long, dark, musty rooms. After a few miles, Cooper finally stopped to open a big oak door and put a hand to the small of her back.

Julia peeked around the door, then walked into the big room rather warily, not too sure what to expect. All the furniture was massive and dark. Then Julia's eyes slowly adjusted to the gloom and she felt herself relax.

Cooper liked to read as much as she did.

Books lay everywhere, old books and new books, on every available surface and lining the walls. Real books, not decorator ones. Julia restrained the urge to go over and look at the titles, although she had a feeling she could get her first real clues to his character if she did.

The only note of warmth was a fire blazing in a huge hearth. Massive oak chairs were grouped around it. Julia could make out the forms of a man and a little boy. The man was black-haired and dressed in black, just like Cooper, and Julia wondered if she had missed out on some new fad—ninja cowboys.

"Miss Andersen!" Rafael leapt out of his seat and came running to her. He lifted a small, anxious face. "Why are you here, Miss Andersen? I didn't do nothing wrong, did I?"

"No, honey," Julia said gently, ruffling his hair. "Of course you didn't do anything wrong. I just came for a visit and to let your daddy know what a good little boy you are." Some of Rafael's anxiety eased, but Julia could still see tension on his face.

Cooper took her arm again and they walked over to the fireplace. "Sally Andersen, I'd like to introduce you to Bernaldo Martinez, Rafael's father and my foreman." The man gave no sign that he heard the words and sat slumped, his head in his hands. "Bernie . . ." Cooper's low voice was a threatening growl.

Slowly, Bernaldo Martinez stood up and turned to Julia. She winced when she saw his eyes. The whites were close to the color of the many traffic lights she'd distractedly run through in her life. She wondered if it hurt to look out of eyes that were so red. The man was haggard, with a few day's worth of stubble on his lean, good-looking face. It wasn't designer stubble, achieved with the use of a special razor, but real stubble which came from not shaving for many days. Probably the same number of days he hadn't been sleeping. "Bernie!" Cooper's voice was, if possible, lower and more threatening than before.

Martinez ran a hand through his hair, then nodded at Julia. "Miss Andersen." His voice was scratchy and rough.

"Mr. Martinez." Julia inclined her head.

"Listen, sport." Cooper hunkered down until he was eye level with Rafael. His voice was gentle again. "Southern Star gave birth last night. Why don't you ask Jacko to take you to see the foal?"

"A foal?" Rafael's face filled with joy, all the tension clearing in an instant. "Yowee!" he screamed, punching the air. Remembering his manners, he murmured a hurried goodbye to Julia, then scrambled out the door.

Bernie Martinez's head slowly swung over to Cooper. It looked as if it hurt him to do it. "What was it? A filly?"

Cooper stood up and pinned Martinez with a hard look. "Colt."

"A colt." Martinez gave a harsh laugh. "Well, congratulations. Another Cooper stud is born."

"That's enough, Bernie." Cooper's voice was so deep and icy Julia shivered.

But Martinez wasn't impressed. "I'll bet if we hadn't moved here, my Carmelita would still be around. I'll bet—"

"I said that's enough!" Cooper stepped toward Martinez, his big hands clenched into fists. Martinez angled his stubbled chin defiantly upward, daring Cooper to take a crack.

There was a heavy, musky smell in the air and Julia wondered if it was from all those books, or from the testosterone. Something had to be done and quickly. Martinez looked like he could barely survive his hangover, let alone a few rounds with Cooper. Julia looked again at his huge hands, now balled into fists. Probably not too many people would survive a few rounds with Cooper.

"Well," Julia said, and rubbed her hands together. "Well, here we are." Getting no reaction from the two males in the room, she attempted a smile.

Nothing.

They just stood there, glowering at each other as if she didn't exist.

She gave up. "Uh, Cooper?" Julia just managed to avoid tugging on his shirtsleeve to get his attention. But that wasn't necessary. Those fierce dark eyes were instantly focused on her. She shivered again, but not from fear.

"I—" Julia licked dry lips. "I left my briefcase in the Blazer, and there's some of Rafael's homework I wanted to show Mr. Martinez. No—" she held up her hand as Cooper started forward. "I'll get it myself, if you'll just refresh my memory about how to get back to the kitchen. Or draw me a map."

Cooper's deep voice was gentle again. "Turn right outside the door, then seven doors down turn left and follow the corridor to the end, then through the pantry and into the kitchen."

Julia was finding it oddly hard to concentrate when he was looking at her so intently. "Seven doors, left, pantry, kitchen," she said, breathlessly. "Right." She turned and walked out the door and looked with dismay down the endless, enormous corridor.

Maybe she should have left a trail of bread crumbs.

When the door closed behind Julia, Bernie collapsed into the chair and scrubbed his face with his hands. He stared into the fire for a long time. Cooper was uncomfortable. Carmelita's leaving had really punched a hole in Bernie's life. But that still didn't excuse his rudeness to Sally Andersen.

"Listen, Bernie," Cooper said, "I understand how you feel, but you've got to pull yourself together. After all, Miss Andersen—"

"Forget her," Bernie said nastily. "I don't have to talk to her."

"Bernie," Cooper said patiently, "shut up. And stop acting crazy."

"I got a right to go crazy," Bernie shouted. "I just lost my wife!"

"Well, can it!" Cooper shouted back. "Miss Andersen is coming back any minute now. She's taken time out to talk to you about your son, and you're damn well going to straighten out and be civil to her."

Bernie tried to focus on Cooper. His eyes glittered an unholy red. "Make me," he growled.

He was spoiling for a fight and the last thing Cooper wanted was for the town's new second grade teacher to walk in on a brawl. "Stop it, Bernie."

"No." Bernie stood up, swayed, then went into a fighting stance, which was ridiculous. He could barely stand on his feet.

"Stop it." Cooper raised his eyes to the ceiling. "We both know you can't beat me hand to hand. I'm trained and you're not. And anyway, I've got five inches and twenty pounds on you. Now cut this out."

Bernie was slowly circling him. "Make me."

"Bernie," Cooper said through gritted teeth. "You're drunk. You're probably seeing double. I'm not going to fight you, and that's that. I'd only take you down—and it would be as easy as a mule breaking wind."

Cooper was expecting Bernie to smile at one of his grandfather's favorite expressions, but Bernie just set his jaw and swung heavily.

Cooper dodged the blow without moving his feet. This was going to be worse than he thought. Bernie swung again, so slowly Cooper still had time to catch Bernie's fist in his hand. Cooper let Bernie wrench his hand free and said, "Don't be a fool, Bernie, you can't win and you know it."

"Oh, yeah?" Bernie, breathing heavily, tried to sweep Cooper's legs from under him. It didn't work, but Cooper caught a sharp blow to the shin. "Damn it! That hurt!"

Bernie showed his teeth. "It was meant to." He dropped to a crouch and started circling Cooper. Cooper backed up.

"Bernie, if you don't quit right this minute—" Then Bernie lunged and Cooper stepped aside. The other man banged first his fist and then his head against the fieldstone hearth. Cooper winced at the sound. Bernie turned around, blood flowing from a cut above his eyebrow and lifted his fists. The knuckles of one hand were bleeding. Cooper sighed and lifted his and the door opened.

Julia stopped on the threshold, wide-eyed, briefcase in hand. The two men—one bleeding, one seriously annoyed—turned their heads and stared at her with surly expressions. She almost laughed because they looked exactly like two of her more rambunctious seven-year-olds who had been in a fight.

"I guess this is male bonding, huh?" she asked.

Six

"Ouch!" Bernie tried to jerk his head away.

"Don't be a wuss." Julia caught his chin and dragged his head back to continue cleaning the small raw-looking laceration on his forehead. "I thought cowboys were supposed to be such tough guys."

"I'm no cowboy," Bernie complained as Julia finished cleaning the wound. "I'm just a poor *cholo* who took courses in animal husbandry 'cause it meant cheap college credits." But he was smiling as he sat at the enormous kitchen table, letting Julia fuss over him. Cooper was smiling too . . . sort of.

Men, thought Julia with exasperation. A quarter of an hour ago they'd been doing their level best to beat each other's brains out, and now look at them. Julia picked up Bernie's hand and looked at his dirty, scraped knuckles. She met Cooper's eyes.

"When was the last time that room was cleaned?"

"It's clean." Cooper felt affronted. "My ranch hands take the cleaning in four-man shifts. They muck out the stables and then they muck out—er—they clean the house. Bernie's not going to get an infection, believe me."

"If you say so." Julia looked dubiously at the cuts. "Still, I'd feel better if I put some disinfectant on those knuckles. Is your first-aid kit still in the pickup?"

"You'd be better off using an antibiotic ointment we have for the horses. It's in a bowl in the refrigerator."

Julia stared at Cooper for a minute to figure out whether or not he was joking, but he looked perfectly serious. She didn't know if he even *could* joke, so she walked over to the huge, industrial-size refrigerator, opened the steel door and simply stared inside.

She had girlfriends in Boston whose condos seemed smaller than the inside of the refrigerator.

"Who does the cooking around here?" She looked over her shoulder. "Paul Bunyan?"

"The men take it—"

"In turns. Right." Julia turned back and examined the contents of the refrigerator. "So where is this horse ointment?"

"In a bowl."

"There are two bowls here, Cooper."

"The green one."

Julia checked the other one and her eyes widened. "And what's in the red one?"

Cooper shrugged. "Lunch?"

"No way," Julia said firmly. She backed out of the refrigerator with the green bowl in her hands and closed the heavy door with her hip. "No way is that stuff food. A mutant life form, perhaps, but definitely not lunch." She drew in a deep breath and coughed. The stuff in the green bowl was either going to cure Bernie or kill him.

"I hope you're ready for this, Mr. Martinez."

"Bernie."

"Okay, Bernie. Ready or not, here it comes." She

applied the smelly ointment to his forehead and knuckles and seized the opportunity to talk to him. "Um—about Rafael. He's not paying attention in class and you should know I've caught him crying more times than I can count."

Bernie sighed. "You're quite right, Miss Andersen—"

"Sally," Julia said, hating herself for having to lie.

"Okay, Sally. The story is this. My wife and I had been—" Bernie started breathing heavily. "We . . . we weren't—" Bernie stopped, unable to continue.

"Getting along?" Julia supplied gently.

Bernie nodded miserably.

"I gathered as much. And Rafael was suffering, wasn't he?"

Bernie nodded again and Julia's heart went out to him. She hadn't personally had any experience with divorce, but she imagined that it would be horribly painful.

Then her eyes slid to Cooper. His wife had left him, too. Had he been in this much pain? He didn't look it. That sharp-angled face might as well have been carved out of a rock, the only sign of life those dark, glittering eyes; and yet, it took Julia an effort to wrench her eyes away from him.

"Bernie." Julia firmly fixed her attention back on the father of her small student. "I think someone should be following Rafael's progress, maybe spending a few afternoons with him, making sure he does his homework . . ."

Bernie looked up, puzzled. Then light dawned on his face. "You're right," he breathed. He reached over and grabbed Julia's hand in gratitude. "You're absolutely right." He pumped Julia's hand enthusiastically, then saw Cooper's scowl and hastily dropped it. "Why didn't I think of that? What a wonderful idea. Thank you, Sally. Thank you so much."

"Oh no," Julia said in dismay. "I didn't mean that I—"

"That's just what Rafael needs." Bernie ran his hands through his already disheveled hair and blew a sigh of relief. "A woman's touch," Bernie mused. "Softness, gentleness but discipline, too. That's just what Rafael needs."

"Ah, Bernie, I don't really think—"

"What a lifesaver," he said simply. "Thank you."

"Okay." Julia gave up with a shake of her head. "If that's what you want."

Bernie reached into his back pocket. "So, how much would you like as payment for the lessons?"

"Put your wallet away." Julia narrowed her eyes, thinking hard. She turned to Cooper. "How good is Rafael with animals?"

"Very," Cooper replied. "He wants to be a vet when he grows up."

"Well"—Julia turned back to Bernie—"that's my price. I want Rafael to help me take care of my dog Fred." *My dog?* she thought. "I want him washed and combed. In exchange, Rafael can come over a couple of afternoons a week after school and I'll go over his homework with him." A thought suddenly occurred to her and she turned to Cooper with wide frightened eyes. "But someone will have to come pick Rafael up. I couldn't possibly . . . there's no way—"

"I'll pick him up in the afternoons," Cooper said. Bernie opened his mouth, looked at Cooper and closed it again. "And you haven't stated your full price yet."

Julia tilted her head and observed Cooper. "I haven't?"

"No."

"What's the rest of my price?"

"Your plumbing needs a complete overhaul, your boiler needs first aid, the second step on your porch needs replacing and that's just for starters."

"You're right." Julia smiled dazzlingly at him. "So tell me. How good a handyman is Rafael?"

"Er . . ." Cooper was slightly taken aback. Was he *flirting* with her? The sensation was so novel, he lost track of what they were saying. Flirting with a pretty woman. In the Cooper kitchen. For as long as he could remember, his kitchen had been a cold and impersonal space where men refueled quickly, then left for work as soon as possible, and that certainly included the grim period of his marriage. But with Sally sitting there, gently bantering with him and Bernie, the kitchen became almost *cozy*.

"Coop?" Bernie was looking at him. "You want me to fix her plumbing?"

"No," Cooper answered, the thought of a hammer in Bernie's hands snapping him back to reality. "I will. You're hopeless with tools or with anything that doesn't move or eat hay. I—"

"Dad! *Dad!*" Rafael ran full tilt into the kitchen and was in his father's arms before the kitchen door had swung shut. "Dad, Southern Star had a colt, and he's a beaut! You just wait till Coop trains him; he's gonna win every prize in sight!" The little boy was hopping up and down with excitement.

"That so?" Bernie smiled down at his son, and Julia relaxed. Bernie Martinez might be hurting, and he might have neglected Rafael while his marriage was breaking up, but there was no denying the fact that he loved his son.

Bernie hugged him. "Well, it looks like you're going to be a very busy little boy from now on, what with looking after the new colt and going over your lessons a couple of afternoons a week with Miss Andersen."

Rafael's head turned sharply and his eyes widened. "I am?"

"Yes," Julia smiled. "If that's okay with you. Of course, you're going to have to help me look after my dog in exchange."

"A dog?" Rafael's face lit up. "Neato! What breed is he?"

Julia looked over at Cooper and saw a faint dent in his cheek. A smile? "Cooper? What breed is Fred?"

"Mixed."

"Yeah. I guess that about sums it up." Julia watched as Bernie and Rafael wrestled good-naturedly. *They'll be okay,* she thought. There really wasn't any reason for her to stay any longer. She should say so to Cooper, tell him he could take her home now. *Just a few more minutes,* she thought, *then I'll ask him.*

"Dad? What's for lunch?" Rafael rubbed his tummy. "I'm starving."

Bernie fingered his bristly chin and shot Cooper a wry look. "I haven't been doing much shopping lately, Coop. Who's on kitchen detail today?"

"Jacko should have been," Cooper answered, "but he had to run into Rupert for some baling wire."

"Well then, who's gonna do the cookin'?" Rafael asked plaintively.

As if pulled by an invisible string, three male faces and three pairs of brown eyes turned to Julia with pathetic expressions, looking so much like Fred had last night that she had to bite her cheeks to keep from smiling.

"Would the three of you like me to cook something for lunch?"

The two adults hesitated politely, but Rafael was too small to worry about anything as trivial as manners. "Awesome! I'll bet you cook real good, Miss Andersen."

"Well," Julia replied. "Cook well. And actually, I'm not a bad cook, if I have something to work with." Her eyes slid to Cooper. "Just not what was in that bowl, though. And I peeked in your vegetable bin. It's disgusting."

"You peeked in my what?" Cooper asked.

Julia sighed. "Never mind." She stood up, feeling unaccountably cheerful at the thought of having lunch with Bernie and Rafael. And, well, Cooper, too. "I'm sure you have a well-stocked freezer. I can't imagine anybody living out in the middle of nowhere without a freezer. Where is it?"

"Don't have one," Cooper replied.

"No?" That stopped her. She tried to imagine turning something, anything she had seen in that refrigerator into food, and failed.

"No." Cooper walked over to her and Julia looked up and met his dark brown eyes which had a faint smile lurking in the depths. "But we do have a locker."

"That was delicious," Rafael said, and mopped up his plate with the last biscuit. "Thanks, Miss Andersen."

"Well, you guys are sure easy to please," Julia

smiled. "Broil a few steaks, nuke some potatoes, then just sit back and rake in the compliments."

It was a bit more elaborate than that, Cooper thought. Sally had walked around the locker in wonderment, cracking jokes about its size and making an inventory of the contents. Then she'd managed to marinate the steaks, whip up some garlic butter for the baked potatoes and make a side dish of ham and peas in no time. She'd even made some biscuits from scratch. Everything had been delicious and, above all, she had made it seem easy. While she moved comfortably around the kitchen, she had kept up a light-hearted conversation. Bernie started losing that haunted look he'd had lately, and Rafael had laughed and scampered like the seven–year-old he was instead of moping around, looking as if all the cares of the world rested on his small shoulders.

They'd eaten a delicious lunch in an easy and relaxed atmosphere.

In the Cooper kitchen.

With a woman.

Impossible.

There was something about Sally Andersen that brightened a room, and Cooper had found himself smiling more in the last half hour than he'd done in the past year. Of course, the atmosphere had been a little spoiled by Bernie, whose eyes kept tracking speculatively back and forth between him and Sally.

"Leave that," Cooper said suddenly, when she made to gather up the dishes. "You've done more than enough."

"Okay." She dusted her hands. "I'm sure glad the two of you have patched things up.

Cooper and Bernie exchanged blank looks. "Patched what up?" Cooper asked.

Julia rolled her eyes in exasperation. "Well, I hate to raise painful memories, but the two of you were at each other's throats a little while ago."

"Oh, that," Cooper said, with a shrug of a broad shoulder. "It didn't mean anything."

"Just getting rid of a little stress," Bernie agreed.

"Men." Julia shook her head. "When I want to relieve stress I do something relaxing, like taking a walk or reading a good book. I don't think of bashing someone's head in. Speaking of which—" She turned to Cooper. "I wanted to ask you something."

"About bashing people's heads in?" Cooper was startled.

"No. About reading." She put her chin on her folded hands and directed the full force of that turquoise gaze at him. "I need to ask you something."

"Anything," Cooper replied immediately, then saw Bernie grinning like a fool, swiveling his head back and forth between the two of them. Unfortunately, Bernie was too far away for a kick under the table.

"Your books," Julia said.

"My what?"

"Books," she sighed. "There isn't anyplace in Simpson to buy books, and I've seen that you have a lot of them. Where do you get your books from?"

"Rupert," he said and saw her wince. "Something wrong? Have you been to Rupert?"

"Well . . ." Julia shrugged her shoulders. "Yes and no. It was my first weekend here and I thought I'd sort of explore a bit." She closed her eyes and shuddered at the memory. "And someone mentioned that Rupert was a nice town and that it was thataway, and they just pointed me down this road that went on and on. So I started driving, not really knowing if I was going in the right direction or not . . ." Julia opened her eyes and glared at Cooper. "Did you know that there are no signposts to Rupert?"

"Probably not," Cooper replied calmly. "But anyone born in Simpson can get to Rupert with his eyes closed."

"Well, I wasn't and I can't." Julia swallowed. "So like I say, I just drove on and on and every time there was a fork in the road, I wondered where I was and it was just so . . . so empty. My car's old and I kept thinking that if I had a flat tire or if the car broke down I would be stuck there forever and then the snows would come and they wouldn't find my body until the spring thaw. And by the time I saw a few houses and this big 'Welcome to Rupert' sign, it was getting dark, so I just turned around and drove straight back." She looked at Cooper with her heart in her eyes. "Is it a nice bookstore?"

"It's okay." Cooper drained his coffee. "Bob's got a good selection. And he'll order anything you want if he doesn't have it in stock. Takes about a week." Cooper stood up. "It's getting late and we've taken up enough of your time. I'll drive you back. Er . . . by the way, would you like to come with me to Rupert next Saturday? I've got some business there."

"You do?" Julia perked up.

"You do?" Bernie asked. "I thought we were going to go over—" Then he saw Cooper's glare and slapped himself on the head. Something Cooper would have liked to have done. Only harder. "Oh, I forgot. You've got that—that important business to take care of. Ri-i-i-i-ight. You just go off to Rupert on Saturday and stay as long as you want." Bernie winked. "All night if necessary."

Cooper took Sally's elbow and reminded himself when he came back to give Bernie a few pointers in discretion.

With a cattle prod.

Something was missing, Julia thought, as she looked out of the Blazer's window so she wouldn't have to look at Cooper. Then again, she didn't have to look at him. He seemed to exert a sort of gravitational pull. It had been the same in the kitchen. He had stayed quietly in his chair, rarely talking, and yet everyone seemed to revolve around him, as if she and Bernie and Rafael had been minor planets to his sun. Bernie deferred to him, Rafael plainly adored him, and she, well, she had trouble keeping her eyes off him.

And she had felt—different, all afternoon. What was it? It was such a hard feeling to pin down. She had felt light-hearted, carefree and safe.

Safe. That was it.

Julia had enjoyed bantering with Rafael and joking with Bernie, who'd shed his earlier truculence. Even Cooper's silence had been an interesting kind of silence. She'd felt a lot of things this afternoon—relief that Rafael was going to be all right, amusement at the men's pathetic gratitude for a little cooking, excitement at the thought of making it to a bookstore, a crazy sort of attraction to Cooper. But she hadn't felt loneliness and above all, she hadn't felt the fear that had been her constant companion for the last two months.

And it was thanks to Cooper. She had no doubt about that. It was impossible to feel fear around him. He had sat in the kitchen, silently watching her out of dark eyes, an oddly reassuring presence. It was like having a huge guard dog watching over her.

She sneaked a look at him. He was squinting against the weak autumn sun, the tanned skin around his eyes lined and weatherbeaten, his angular cheekbones oddly elegant in profile. The late afternoon light picked out the few silver hairs in the jet-black mane.

Well, maybe not a guard dog so much as a battle-scarred wolf.

But he was here and she felt watched over, protected by his very presence.

He felt her gaze and flicked a glance her way. She gave him a dazzling smile.

The black Blazer swerved slightly. "What?" he asked.

"Just a smile, Cooper," Julia said, astonished at how safe and free she felt with him. "For no reason at all."

Julia looked back out the window and for the first time allowed herself to really *see* the countryside. The trip to Rupert had been such a nightmare. She hadn't seen anything at all of the landscape itself. All she had done was to crouch anxiously over the steering wheel, painfully aware of the fact that the long prairie grass would easily hide a potential gunman. The lonely stretches of road had been almost designed for ambushes. It had been easy enough to imagine a murderer lurking behind every tree. By the time she had reached Rupert, she had been bathed in sweat.

Now that her fear had abated, she could see that

the countryside had a kind of raw, untamed splendor. A strong wind sent light fluffy clouds scurrying across the pale blue sky, and the scale of the landscape was so vast that she could follow the shadows of the clouds as they raced across the grass.

Cooper pulled up in front of Julia's house and braked to a stop. "Here we are."

"Well," Julia began, "thanks for driving me—"

But Cooper was already circling the Blazer. In an instant, he was at her door with a large, outstretched hand. It was a long step down from the cabin of the vehicle and she appreciated the support of his hand. Once down, she lifted her eyes to his, and again felt like falling toward him. He was safety and excitement and a host of other feelings she couldn't sort out. With the exception of fear. She felt no fear at all.

For the second time in twenty-four hours, Cooper held her hand in his. It still felt small and soft, but at least this time it wasn't cold and trembling. He was grateful for that. He was grateful for a lot of things— the carefree afternoon, the way she seemed to take him in her stride, the way she'd managed to put Bernie and Rafael at their ease. He'd been worried about them, but he knew that today was a turning point for them both.

He wanted to say this to Sally Andersen, tell her what she'd accomplished, how grateful he was, but he couldn't find the words, certainly not any words that wouldn't sound stiff and formal and put distance between them.

With a start, Julia realized that her hand was still in his. Almost reluctantly, she withdrew it.

"Would you—" Her throat was suddenly dry.

"Would you like to come in for some coffee?" Her mouth quirked.

"Can't," Cooper said with regret. He stuck his hands in his jeans pockets, so he wouldn't reach out for her again. Running into town in the afternoons to pick up Rafael would eat into his time, so he needed to get as much done this weekend as possible. And he also wanted to take the time to repair her plumbing—

A cold nose nudged his hand.

Cooper knelt. "Hi there, big boy," he murmured. The dog wriggled happily, then tried to lick his hand. "Hold still now." Cooper ran his hands over Fred's body. The wound on the animal's haunch was healing nicely and the swelling in the right foreleg was going down.

"Oh, dear," she said.

"What's the matter?"

"I was supposed to pick up some dog food today, but I completely forgot." Julia looked down dubiously at Fred, then laughed as he almost knocked her over. "Hey, I'm glad to see you, too." She patted Fred and sighed. "I'm afraid I just don't know that much about dogs. What do they usually eat? Last night I gave him some leftover tuna casserole."

"Judging by today's lunch, I'd say just about anything you cook for him would be all right."

"Yeah?" Julia fondled Fred's ears. "I was planning on a salad tonight."

"In that case, cook him up a mess of rice; that'll do him." Cooper stood up. "We buy kibble wholesale in ten-pound sacks. I'll bring some over on Monday."

"Thanks." Julia looked up at him. He was leaving and it seemed as if the day had dimmed a little.

"No, I should thank you," Cooper shifted uncomfortably. He'd grown so used to feeling ill at ease around people, but this afternoon had been unusually relaxing. However, now he felt stiff and awkward again. All the words he'd like to say, how much he appreciated what she was doing for Bernie and Rafael, how much he'd enjoyed her cooking lunch for them, even how incredibly pretty she looked in the weak dying afternoon sunlight—no, he really couldn't say *that*—froze on his tongue.

He'd be willing to bet even money that Sally Andersen's words never froze on her tongue. There was nothing cold about her. She just let loose with that killer smile and the whole world probably just smiled right back. Except him. He'd forgotten how to talk, how to smile. He was good for nothing now, other than dogs and horses.

He was staring and he knew it. He had to get out before he made things worse, so he nodded and turned and walked away.

Julia stood watching as Cooper climbed gracefully into the cab of the Blazer and drove off. Long after the noise of the Blazer's engine had faded in the cold fall air, she stared after the vehicle in bemusement.

What on earth had happened? They'd been having this perfectly normal conversation—well, what passed for normal conversation with Cooper, one word to her ten—and then he'd just clammed up, turned on his heel and driven away into the sunset.

Fred nudged her knees and her hand dropped absently to his head. "Was it something I said? Something I did?" He whined and licked her hands. "What on earth was that about?"

Fred woofed gently.

"I don't either," she sighed and held the door open for him.

Seven

Julia bolted up in bed, trembling and sweaty. She looked around her room, dry-mouthed and disoriented. She was in Simpson, Idaho. She was safe. There were no killers here. Yet.

She wrapped her arms around herself, shivering. The nightmarish images were fading fast, but the cold remained. Something had happened to the heating system again.

Suddenly, Julia felt alone. Not just alone in her house, but cosmically alone, as if she were the last human being left on the face of the earth. A stirring in the corner of her bedroom sent her heart into her throat. She was reaching for the bedside lamp with some insane thought of hurling it at the intruder when she heard a snuffle.

Surely crazed murderers didn't snuffle.

"Fred?" she said softly, peering into the darkness. She turned on the bedside lamp. There was the scrabble of doggy claws on the hardwood floor. Maybe she really was the last human being left on this earth, but at least she wasn't going to be the last living creature. Fred laid his muzzle on the bed and whined.

"Okay." Julia patted the covers and made room for him as he jumped on the bed. "But only for tonight, is that clear?" She was speaking to herself, because Fred had curled into a ball at her side and was already fast asleep. His big body made the mattress sag a bit, but she didn't care.

It was hard not to think how much more comforting it would be to have a man in her bed. A strong man who would wrap her in his arms and tell her not to worry her pretty little head about anything, because he was there.

Someone like, say, Cooper.

But that was nuts. Cooper wouldn't really talk to her.

Julia turned off the lights and snuggled into the warmth of the covers and wrinkled her nose. On the other hand, Cooper probably wouldn't be furry and smelly.

"Whoa there!"

Monday evening, Julia laughed and wiped soap out of her eyes. She watched as Rafael coaxed a dripping Fred out of the tub. She raised her hands to shield herself from the spray as the dog shook himself vigorously.

"You still smell, buddy." Julia took a deep breath and handed an old towel to Rafael. She capped her bottle of bubble bath. "But at least there's this whiff of roses over the Eau de Dog."

Julia ran her hands over Fred's still damp fur. Clean, he looked almost good. She lifted her head as a deep pounding sounded from outside her door. Trembling with fright, Julia rose and rushed to the door. If anyone had come for her, they would find Rafael . . . She jerked the door open.

"Oh, hi, Cooper." She slumped with relief against

the frame, thankful that her knees would hold her weight.

Cooper looked up the steps and nodded, and for once she understood why he didn't speak to her: His mouth was full of nails.

Cooper was sitting on the bottom step. Julia tried not to notice his incredibly long legs stretched out onto the cracked sidewalk, with about the same success she had not noticing how his broad shoulders stretched the seams of his black shirt. She was so acutely aware of his physical presence that she was almost tempted to turn on her heels and go back into the house, back to little Rafael and stinky Fred, neither of whom posed any danger to her self-control. But the manners her mother had drilled into her stopped her from it. And besides, this was her year for living dangerously.

So she walked down to the bottom step and sat down, frowning because something wasn't quite right.

The second step hadn't creaked.

"Hey," she said, pleased, "you fixed the step. Thanks."

Cooper nodded and pulled the nails from his mouth. "How's the heating working?"

Julia sighed. "Right now it's okay, but Saturday night it went out and it went out again yesterday afternoon for a few hours."

Cooper frowned. "Probably a faulty contact. I'll look at it for you, then I have to take Rafael home."

"Thanks." Julia brushed a few dog hairs from the hem of her skirt. "It's really nice of you. You don't have to do all this, you know." She looked up but

Cooper was already gone. She sighed and got up to follow him into the house.

She stood in her small front parlor. She could hear Rafael and Fred making a mess in the bathroom, and Cooper doing something manly and competent in the pantry. She might as well go do something womanly and competent in the kitchen.

"Well, that should take care of it." Cooper walked out of the pantry, wiping his hands on a rag.

Julia looked up and smiled. "Good. Thanks so much. There's nothing worse than a cold house." She pulled back a kitchen chair. "You've got one more task before you go, Cooper. I want you to taste my lemon tart."

Cooper sat down, picked up his fork and cut off a large pale yellow bite.

Julia watched him anxiously. Cooper chewed slowly and she just managed to stop herself from fidgeting. "Well?" she asked, finally.

Cooper finished it off in several bites. "Good," he said and took a sip of the steaming cup of tea she had placed next to his plate. "Good," he said again and looked up at her.

Good, he grunts, Julia thought in exasperation. It was her mother's secret recipe for tarte au citron, famous in over three states, and all the man could say was good? It happened to be fabulous, and the least he could do was say so.

Julia opened her mouth to make a sarcastic crack, then stopped.

It was totally unfair what the man could do to her, simply sitting at her kitchen table, big hands curled around her flowered tea cup. He looked so incredibly large and—and male. It wasn't fair that she found his face so compelling when Cooper wasn't even handsome.

But there it was. She could feel her heart pounding in her chest and she busied herself with the remaining pie. "Here." She thrust a package into Cooper's hands. "I wrapped half the pie in tinfoil for Rafael and Bernie to eat later."

"They'll like that." Cooper stood up suddenly and Julia took a step backward. He seemed to fill her entire small kitchen. "Thanks."

"Don't mention it." Julia gathered the plates and put them in the sink. "You fixed my heating system. Believe me, I'd do more than bake a pie for hot water and heat."

"Hi, Coop." Rafael walked in and blew wet bangs out of his face. He looked bedraggled and happy. "I'm ready to go."

Cooper put a big hand on Rafael's shoulder and turned the boy gently toward Julia. "Before we go, sport, don't you think you should say—" His gaze lifted and his eyes met hers and again, Julia had that helpless, drowning feeling. "Thanks," he murmured.

"Golly, yeah, Miss Andersen. Fred and me had a great time."

"Miss Andersen's baked a pie and she wrapped half of it up for you." Cooper nudged Rafael gently. "You'll be wanting to thank her for that, too."

"Pie?" Rafael's eyes lit up and he swiveled to Julia. "Thanks, Miss Andersen."

"This is really nice of you." Cooper hefted the wrapped package. It was still warm and he suddenly thought how warm everything about Sally Andersen was. Warm pie, warm smile, warm woman—Cooper had to look away or he'd start staring again. "We usually buy a gross of frozen ones and thaw 'em out now and again in the microwave. Rafael and Bernie'll really appreciate it. We don't get too many home-made pies out at the ranch."

Not too many homemade pies, Cooper thought, *and not too many homemade meals.* The ranch was a motherless, wifeless, womanless place.

"We have to go," he said abruptly and turned and ushered Rafael out.

By this time, Julia was getting used to his abrupt leavetakings. Who knew? Maybe elaborate goodbyes were considered citified. Still, without admitting to herself that she wanted one last look at him, she pushed open the screen door and watched as Cooper hoisted Rafael up onto the passenger seat. As always, his movements were precise, graceful.

Though his shirt and jeans looked perfectly clean, they also looked exactly like what he had been wearing on Saturday. He was climbing into a black mini-van she hadn't seen before.

Julia wondered about a man who seemed to have more vehicles than clothes.

Shopping at Jensen's was becoming a pleasant ritual.

"Here, honey," Loren Jensen said to his wife, "you can start bagging these." He ticked off the items slowly, but Julia knew better than to fret. If truth be told, she was even starting to sort of, well, *enjoy* the slower pace of Simpson.

"Yogurt, milk, eggs, bread—say, ever since you started ordering that oatmeal bread, I've got more and more people asking for it." Loren smiled at Julia and turned to his wife. "Isn't that right, honey?"

"You bet. We're going to try the supplier's bran-nut bread next week. And we sold out that yogurt you ordered, too. You're not our best customer—you don't eat enough to keep a bird alive, Sally—but you're sure our smartest customer." Beth Jensen, an ample, middle-aged woman with kindness etched on her face, picked up the wrapped loaf, and carefully positioned it next to the carton of eggs. "There you go, dear. Just walk carefully, don't jitterbug down the street and you'll be fine."

"Thanks, Beth." Julia smiled at her and bent to pick up the two grocery sacks. "I'll be careful, I promise. After all the trouble you've gone to for me—"

"No trouble at all, honey," Loren replied. "Are you sure you got everything you need? You might want to add some cookies if you've got Rafael coming over afternoons." He narrowed his eyes and tapped his lip as his eyes swept around the store.

"Sure," Julia said, marveling all over again at the pace at which small-town gossip got around. She put the bags back down on the counter. "Go ahead and add some cookies. What do you suppose Rafael likes?"

"Oreos," Beth said and pulled a package from a nearby shelf. "Well, that seems to be it. Oh!" She reached out and placed a six-pack of beer on top of Julia's groceries. "Almost forgot this."

"But, but, I don't want beer," Julia protested. She preferred wine, though one sip of Loren's jug wine had left what felt like a permanent hole in her stomach. She'd steered clear of it ever since. "I don't particularly like beer."

"It's not for you, dear," Beth said easily. "It's for Cooper. That's his favorite brand. Coming over afternoons, helping you fix up your house. That's thirsty work. And who knows?" She gave Julia a conspiratorial wink. "Maybe a little beer might relax him a bit."

"I—" Julia felt her face flame. "Oh, no, it's nothing like—I mean, he and I aren't . . . in any way—" For the first time in living memory, words defeated her. Her tongue disconnected completely from her brain and flapped around uselessly in her mouth.

Loren looked disapprovingly at his wife. "Coop's a good man."

Beth sighed. "I know he's a good man, you ninny. I've known him as long as you have. He's too good a man to be on his own." She gave her husband a wifely look. "He just needs a little nudge in the right direction."

Eight

Cooper remembered reading somewhere that scientists had figured out why some people were considered beautiful. It was a trick played on the mind by geometry. Beauty was symmetry; it was as simple as that. If the two sides of the face were equal—bingo! Movie star or cover girl.

Cooper risked a glance at the woman sitting beside him. One front tooth was slightly crooked and her right eyebrow had a higher arch than the left. Most of the time her smile was lopsided. Technically speaking, Sally Andersen wasn't beautiful.

So why couldn't he keep his eyes off her? Maybe it was because wherever she was, there was a vibrancy in the air, like around a hummingbird. There was a glow to her, as if she were lit from within. As if all he had to do was hold out his hands and the coldness he felt inside would dissipate.

It was a good thing he could drive to Rupert blindfolded because he was so easily distracted by the emotions that crossed her expressive face, everything up-front, in vivid Technicolor. Her coloring was so exquisite, from the pearly perfection of her skin with faint peach undertones, to the deep turquoise eyes and the finely arched auburn brows.

The only thing dull about her was her hair, which was a nondescript brown, and he thought he was lucky there. He'd always loved red hair on a woman, and if Sally Andersen's hair had been red, he would have been a goner.

He was halfway there already.

But it wasn't her looks that kept him hovering around her like a lovesick puppy. He'd been around beautiful women before. Melissa herself was no slouch in the looks department. But with Melissa, he could feel the coldness—which had been a part of him for as long as he could remember—starting to set, threatening to encase him in ice forever.

There was no ice around Sally Andersen. She simply reached out and warmed his heart.

Cooper wondered with deep unease whether she found his silences offensive or strange. Melissa had complained loudly and often about his silences, accusing him of ignoring her. He had felt himself drawing further away from his wife, as her complaints increased in tone and intensity, until finally she left him to his silence and solitude.

Sally was a talker. Ordinarily, that would irritate him. He was a loner by temperament and by inclination, but he found himself drawn in by her gentle voice as she talked about her week. Articulate and amusing, she was a delight to listen to. There was no malice in her, either. And best of all, so far she wasn't showing any sign of being put off by his silences, as most people seemed to be.

Then, as he listened to her, he grew more and more astounded as she described her dealings with the people in Simpson. Was it possible that there were two different towns with the same name? How could he have been in the same places at the same time as she had, and not noticed what was going on? She told him all about the lives of people he'd known for years. How could she know so much? And why didn't he know it? As he listened to her talk about the people he had grown up with, he was amazed and a little saddened. Why didn't anyone ever say anything to him?

Where had he been while all this was going on?

For a while there, as Cooper drove her through the wilderness, Julia wondered why Cooper wasn't talking to her. Maybe it was because she was a woman. She kept stealing quick glances at his hard, craggy face and finally decided that he was probably an equal-opportunity non-speaker.

Julia had kept herself busy, mostly, in Simpson. School, Rafael, Fred. Meddling in other people's affairs. Most of the time it worked to keep her fears at bay. At times, though—like now—reality intruded. She looked out through the windows of the Blazer and felt chilled. The landscape was as empty as her soul, as her life.

Julia tried hard not to think about what would happen to her life. Later. After the trial, if she made it that far, she wouldn't really have a life to go back to.

If she got back.

She knew perfectly well that her job wouldn't be waiting for her when she returned. Oh, Warwick Publishing might keep her on, if the government made a fuss about it, but it would be some insignificant, paper-pushing job, not the editing position she'd attained before.

For better or worse, her life in Simpson *was* her life now.

She shivered and barely noticed when Cooper bent to turn on the heating system. She wasn't cold outside; she was cold inside. Cold and miserable and lonely. And scared.

Still, as long as she was in a moving vehicle with Cooper, she felt reasonably safe. She didn't need to look across to the steering wheel to know that his hands were large and competent, that he was tall and strong, and that he seemed to know how to do just about anything. If they had a flat tire, he could probably hold the vehicle up with a rope held between his teeth and change the tire while fending off marauders. He was, after all, a trained soldier. And to top it all off, there was even a rifle in the Blazer, and Cooper had said that he knew how to use it.

Then again, he had also said he was better with a knife.

Julia shuddered at the direction her thoughts had taken. She felt completely lost and alone, out of her depth. *What was she doing here?* In Simpson she was a stranger, in the most literal sense of the term. She wanted to drown her black, bleak thoughts, but she didn't have anything to drown them in—not a good book, not even some whisky.

All she had was Cooper.

"Cooper?"

"Yeah?"

"Talk to me." Julia could hear the wistful note in her voice. So many things had been taken from her. *Talk to me,* she thought. *Let me feel connected to the human race. Make me feel less alone and scared.*

"Talk to you?" Julia could hear the tension in Cooper's voice. "What do you want me to talk about?"

"Oh, I don't know. Your family."

"Er . . ." he said, and wrenched his eyes away from her. It wasn't that he didn't want to talk to her.

The problem was her face. She had an odd beauty he found highly distracting. Like the line of her cheekbone. And her nose, small and perfect. And those eyes. Sally's irises were striated in stunning greens and blues which blended to look like turquoise. He hadn't noticed that before.

"Cooper?" Her voice sounded worried. "You still there?"

They had just passed the Berndt spread. That meant that they were ten minutes out from Rupert. Seven if he hurried. He stepped on the accelerator.

"I told you about my great-grandfather, didn't I?"

Julia nodded and looked around. They seemed to have picked up speed. "The guy who built that great big house?"

"Right." Cooper watched the telephone poles whiz by. "He came out West in 1887 and was granted the statutory hundred-and-thirty acres. Once he proved his claim, he got himself a mail-order bride. They say she was very beautiful. He fell in love with her. She was Irish, like him. Her parents had brought the family to America during the potato famine, but then they were both taken ill with influenza and died. She was left on her own at sixteen and she saw his ad in a newspaper. It was either marry a man she'd never met before or starve. He sent her the money and she traveled West. The problems began almost immediately. It seems that my great-grandfather was a difficult man. A . . . taciturn man."

You don't say, Julia thought. "Well," she said kindly, "a glib tongue isn't everything."

Cooper shot her a questioning glance. "No, I suppose not. Still, the people in Simpson could tell that things were going badly."

"Simpson existed even back then?"

"Yeah." Cooper's eyes shifted left and right. They were nearing the outskirts of Rupert. "It was just a hole in the wall back then."

As opposed to the bustling metropolis it is today, Julia thought wryly. After a moment or two of silence, she gave him a verbal nudge. "So . . . we have your great-grandfather who wasn't much of a talker and his beautiful wife. They're not getting on. They have a child. A boy."

Cooper's head jerked around. "You already know the story," he said accusingly.

"Nope." She sent him a smug smile. "You told me that much. Besides, if they hadn't had a child you wouldn't be here now, telling me all about it, would you?"

"No, I guess not." Cooper hated the next bit. But she'd asked and he was honor-bound to tell her. "Anyway, to cut a long story short, she stayed just long enough to wean Ethan—"

"Your grandfather."

Cooper nodded. "My grandfather. Just long enough to wean him and ensure that he would survive. He was two when my great-grandmother ran off. She just up and went one day; nobody knows where."

"Didn't your great-grandfather try to track her down?"

"No. They say he never saw her again."

"Wow." Julia was busy trying to fit all these details

into the image she had of Cooper. "Did he ever re-marry?"

"No. He just kept working the farm and making a little more money each year. Then he decided to import some stallions. That was the beginning of the Cooper stud farm."

"Then you're a fourth-generation breeder." *And a fourth-generation non-talker.* Maybe he was genetically unable to chitchat.

"Yeah." Cooper allowed himself a small smile. "We're fairly well-known."

That was an understatement. Loren Jensen had told her that the Cooper stud farm was one of the best in the country. "So what happened next?"

Cooper should have known she wouldn't let it go. He stalled. "What do you mean?"

"Cooper." Julia threw him a reproachful glance. "Did your great-grandmother die and haunt the property or something? Or maybe—"

"No, she just never came back. Either in the flesh or in the spirit."

"So then what happened?"

Cooper sighed. "Then my grandfather grew up and inherited the farm and imported more horses. He was the one who started breeding scientifically. He was one of the first in this country to apply the new science of genetics to horse breeding. He imported three Arabians in 1912—"

"Cooper . . ." Julia said in exasperation, "I'm not all that interested in horses."

"Oh." He pursed his lips. "Yeah. Well, my grandmother had my father and after five years of marriage, she ran away with the Singer man." He pulled quickly into a parking spot. "She took the sewing machine with her."

"And your mother died when you were small," Julia said slowly. "And . . . and your wife left you. Sounds almost like a jinx of some kind."

He was at the passenger door and had her hand in his. She stepped down. He was tempted to tuck her hand into his arm, but didn't. "Well . . ." He looked around for help or at least a distraction, but the street was empty. "Some people call it that. They say that no woman—no female—can live on the Double C ranch. That the Double C is cursed to be womanless. By some fluke, we also breed more colts than fillies." He put a hand to her back and they started walking. He wanted to get her to Bob Dolan's Corner Bookshop as quickly as possible.

She was silent as they crossed the street. On the other side, she looked up at him with a frown of concentration, clear turquoise eyes trained on him. When he met her gaze, Cooper had the feeling she was seeing straight into his soul. "That's it?" she asked. "You didn't leave anything out? No wailing ghosts, no clanking chains?"

"Nope."

"Just women who run away from Cooper men?"

Cooper winced. "That's about the size of it."

Julia turned it all over in her mind. "Hmm," she said thoughtfully, "I think that's ridiculous."

"You—what?" Cooper stared.

"So there have been some troubled marriages in your family. So what? That's not a jinx. That's life."

He stopped suddenly, right in the middle of the sidewalk. "Do you mean that?"

"Sure I do." She blinked and smiled. Her smile

was lopsided. It was asymmetrical. It melted him. "A jinx," she said, waving her hand dismissively. "That's the silliest thing I ever heard."

"Good. I think so, too." Cooper felt as if a great weight had been lifted off his chest. "Let's get going, then. You'll want some time in the bookshop. Then I know a good place for lunch."

"Good story, isn't it?" Cooper asked quietly. "Just shows what the human spirit can endure."

Julia looked up, confused. She had to wrench her attention back to the here and now. She had been totally immersed in Song Li's story of Vietnam in the early nineteen-sixties. It was a riveting book already in the first few pages.

"Have you read it?"

Cooper nodded. He put down the pile of books he was carrying and picked it up. "I read it when it first came out. Nam was a hellhole then. It's a wonder the woman survived to tell the tale." His face was remote, unsmiling, as if he were remembering something horrible.

"Oh, Cooper," Julia breathed. She hadn't really thought . . . and yet she should have. And now a lot of things about Cooper made sense. She stepped closer and put a hand on his arm. It was like touching iron. "Was it—was it bad?"

Cooper looked down at her hand. He could feel the warmth of it through his shirt and jacket. "Was what bad?"

"The war, of course. But that's stupid of me. Of course it was bad. Dear God, it must have been sheer hell."

Cooper didn't mind her hand on his arm at all. But it shouldn't be there under false pretenses. "Are you talking about the Vietnam War, Sally?" he asked.

"Well, of course," she said, confused.

"I was twelve when Saigon fell," he said as gently as he could. He thought for a moment. "I wasn't in the Korean War, either. Or World War II."

Julia added and subtracted and felt foolish. "Oh. Right." She shook her head and her hand dropped. "Sorry about that. I guess I got my dates all wrong."

His lips curved. "That's all right."

"But—" Julia tilted her head and looked at Cooper. His longish black hair was brushed back. His suit was beautifully cut. His tie was silk and echoed the silk square in his jacket pocket. Today, he looked like what he was—a prosperous businessman. Despite the elegant suit and the polished loafers, however, he still looked every inch a warrior. "Chuck Pedersen said you'd been awarded a medal. What was it for, then? Desert Storm?"

"No, I'd quit by then. My father passed away in 1990 and I had to take over the ranch."

"So, what was it? What war were you in?" Had she missed a war somewhere between college and Boston?

"No war." Cooper pulled in a deep breath. In his nightmares, he could still smell burning diesel fuel and cordite. "Flight 101," he said grimly.

"Cooper!" Julia was stunned. Wars were remote events, played out somewhere far away. Flight 101 had been hijacked on American soil—at JFK airport, not ten miles from where she had just started her studies at Columbia. She had watched the tragedy of Flight 101 unfold on CNN. The whole coun-

try had remained glued to their TV sets for four days and four nights, praying for the hostages. Everyone had followed the terrifying sequence of events live: the terrorists' demands, the stalled negotiations and the horrible sight of seven of the hostages being shot from the open cockpit, their bodies dropped on the tarmac one by one. "That little girl." Julia's stomach clenched at the memory. "Were you there when . . . when—" She couldn't say it.

"Yes, I was there. We'd been called in immediately. We had orders to wait for negotiations to pan out. We waited and we waited. When the little girl was—" Cooper looked away and his jaw muscles worked. "That's when we decided to move."

She remembered the men in black ski masks who had swarmed into the plane on the runway. So one of them had been Cooper. "That's what you got the medal for," Julia said.

"Mm-hm." Cooper looked around. "You about ready to go?"

"Yes, I think so." Julia was still struggling with what he had told her. It was one thing to know a man who had been to war. It was quite another to have *seen* him on TV doing it. Of course, he had been wearing a ski mask at the time. And of course, she hadn't known him then.

At the time, Julia suddenly remembered, she had been dating Henry Borsello, a history major. He had been charming and chatty and shallow, the very opposite of Cooper. For a moment, Julia tried to imagine Henry in a ski mask taking out terrorists with machine guns, or even fixing her plumbing. She failed miserably.

"Let's go have lunch then, Cooper," she said. "It's not every day a girl gets to have lunch with a real live hero."

Nine

"Talk to me, Cooper," Julia said before taking another bite of her chiliburger.

"Okay." Cooper signaled for another beer to gain time, but when he looked back, there she was, watching him out of those clear, beautiful eyes. "You like it here?"

Julia put her burger down carefully and looked around the Brewery. It had stained hardwood floors. Against one wall was a working fireplace and the merrily burning logs added coziness and warmth. It was decorated with old copper pots as planters and a wagon wheel as a chandelier.

"It's great," she said softly, watching him expectantly.

His turn now.

"Er . . ."

"I guess you're not too good at this talking thing," she said.

"No." Cooper concentrated on his Mexican omelette. It was delicious, but all of a sudden it tasted like sawdust. He could feel his shoulder muscles tense.

The waitress slipped another pint of beer in front of him, and he sipped it and eyed her warily.

"How come it's so nice here?" Julia asked.

Cooper had been prepared to be stoic, but he felt his composure slip slightly. "I beg your pardon? Nice where?"

"Here. In Rupert." Julia waved her arm, encompassing the warm café and the town outside. "This place is great. The food is wonderful. The decor is authentic. It's a truly great little café. Bob Dolan's Corner Bookshop was wonderful, too. It was a perfect small-town bookstore. We walked down two perfect small-town streets to get here and they were planted with larch and geraniums. Rupert could be in a guide book. Great Small Towns of the West." She folded her hands under her chin. "So what went wrong with Simpson?"

It was a good question. And a smart one, too. Cooper turned it over in his mind.

"Well, maybe towns are like people. Some are hardy and some aren't. Some withstand hardship better than others. Horses are like that, too," he added after a moment.

"When did Simpson start to . . . ah . . ." Julia tried to find a word that wouldn't be too strong, "decline?"

Cooper paused to consider. "Guess maybe the death knell was when the new interstate ran forty miles west of Simpson. That was back in 1972."

"You mean surveyors draw a line in the map for a road and a town goes down the drain—" Julia snapped her fingers, "like that?"

"Yeah. But then that's how most towns in the West were founded anyway, so I suppose it's poetic justice."

"What do you mean?"

This was his terrain and Cooper relaxed. The history of the West was something he knew a lot about. He leaned back and watched her. Sally had finished her chiliburger and was eagerly picking up the last French fry. It was firm and crisp and when she put it in her mouth she closed her eyes to savor the taste. She ate like she did everything, with delight and total concentration. She licked her lips and opened her eyes suddenly and he realized that he had been staring. He had been staring at her mouth and at her pink tongue as she licked her lips, imagining what it would feel like to run his own tongue over those lips. He felt something stir that hadn't stirred in a long, long time.

"Cooper?" Julia concentrated on breathing in and out and not on what had flashed in Cooper's eyes for just a second. Something intense. Something hot and dangerous.

"You want anything else?" Cooper asked her and she tore her gaze from his to look blindly at the menu and order dessert at random. By the time the waitress had walked away with an order for cheesecake, carrot cake, muffins and coffee for two, she had herself under control.

What had happened back there? It had been like looking into a furnace.

Julia leaned to the left as the waitress placed their order in front of them, then concentrated on what Cooper was saying.

"Most of the towns out here were founded on a whim—where a miner happened to pitch a tent, or where a settler was buried, or where there was groundwater. In Montana and Wyoming, it was even more arbitrary. The railway engineers just took a pencil and a compass and marked off fifty-mile lengths along the tracks for where the trains needed to load up with water and that's where they founded the railway towns. Likely as not, the towns were named after the engineer's mother or wife or daughter. There are a lot of towns named Clarissa and Lorraine out there. Some grew, some didn't. Simpson was luckier than most, for a while, anyway. For a while there was cattle, and that was profitable until the railway changed its route. Since then there's been a slow decline."

"That's fascinating." Julia cut into the carrot cake. It was fragrant and moist. She speared a morsel. It was delicious, made with whole-meal flour, but that wasn't what held her attention. Cooper did.

"You grew up near a ghost town yourself."

"I did?" Julia stopped, her fork halfway to her mouth.

"Shanako," Cooper looked at her expectantly.

Julia was baffled. "Shanawhat?"

Cooper cut into his cheesecake. "Shanako. A famous ghost town. Largest sheep exporter in the world until the Australian market opened up in the 1860s, then it just dropped off the map. Went from 40,000 people to zero in a year. Don't tell me you've never been there. It can't be more than 70 miles from Bend."

She was smiling politely, as if Cooper had suddenly, inexplicably lapsed into Urdu. Cooper frowned. "Didn't Chuck say you came from Bend, Oregon?"

Where had she heard that name, Bend—Of course! Her cover story. Herbert Davis had drilled her hastily before her departure. *You are now Sally Andersen. Your parents are Roy and Sandra Andersen, of Bend, Oregon. You are a grade school teacher.* Suddenly she couldn't remember the rest. She was so intent on Cooper that there wasn't room for anything else. Her brain simply stalled.

"Sally?" Cooper was looking at her strangely.

"Who?" she said. Then—"Oh!" She shook herself and tried to replay in her head the last few minutes of conversation. "No, I—I've never been to . . . Shanako. We moved to Bend when I was in—" her mind raced, "in junior high, then I went to college in—" *Where would an Oregonian go to college?*

"Portland?" Cooper was watching her, his dark eyes piercing.

"Right," Julia said. This was such a strain. Why hadn't Herbert Davis issued her an instruction manual for being undercover? "So I guess I haven't explored as much around Bend as I should have." Cooper was watching her with an intent gaze. His dark eyes had the ability to throw her for a loop, no doubt about it. She changed the subject. "So what about Simpson? You said the interstate was moved, and I suppose it makes sense that the move would have an impact on Simpson. There'd be less traffic going through town. Anything else?"

"Yeah." Cooper finished off his bite and lifted up another forkful of the fluffy cheesecake. "Well, you can't get food like this in Simpson."

Julia nodded. She had sampled the fare at the town diner and it had been bad enough to cause the demise of a town all by itself.

"There just isn't anyplace decent in town to eat. Wish someone would buy the place, but no one wants to take over a business like that anymore. Can't turn a profit."

"Mmm." Julia sipped her coffee and wasn't surprised to find that it was one of the best cups of coffee she'd ever had. The Brewery was truly a fantastic café. 'Lee Kellogg isn't going to take over Glenn's hard-

ware store," Julia continued. "He wants to be a history teacher, instead. Glenn is thinking of selling in
a few years. Particularly since Maisie isn't interested
in helping out in the store."

Cooper gaped. Where did she *get* this stuff?

Julia didn't notice Cooper's astonishment and was
blithely chatting as she finished off a muffin. "Actually, Beth Jensen says that what Maisie would really
like to do is be a cook. But who could hire a cook in
Simpson?"

"Nobody." Cooper signaled the waitress for the
check. "Businesses aren't doing too well in Simpson."

"It's the broken window theory." Julia watched
Cooper getting ready to pay for lunch. She moved
her bag a few strategic inches closer.

"The what?"

"Broken window theory. I read about it in a maga-
zine. They did this study on slums and housing proj-
ects. Some low-income neighborhoods are kept up by
the residents and some become a wasteland. All it
takes in a housing project is one broken window for
the place to degenerate. It's like a symbol that no one
cares. A license for everyone to trash the place."

"Yeah." Cooper nodded thoughtfully. "I guess
Simpson's a bit like that. No one has done anything
up in a long time. Shops have been closing for ten
years and no one's investing in the place. The town
won't last too long if someone doesn't do something.
Places need attention, just like people."

Julia signaled the waitress for the check. She
rounded on Cooper when she heard him start to protest. "I don't want to hear a word out of you, Cooper.
Not one word. You've been kind enough to drive me

out here and show me around. I won't let you pay
for lunch. This is my treat." She smiled as Cooper
glowered. "After all, Cooper, this is the nineties." She
thought of his penchant for local history. "The *nine-
teen* nineties."

Cooper kept waiting for Sally to ask him to talk on
the ride back. And when she did, he would. He already had a few opening gambits. He was ready. All
she had to do was ask.

But she wasn't asking. Actually, she wasn't doing
much of anything on the other side of the Blazer's
cabin, aside from looking out the window lost in
thought.

Silence was Cooper's companion, something he
was familiar with, something he could handle. Some-
how, though, silence and Sally Andersen were two
things that didn't seem to go together at all. He
found himself craving her attention. He missed her
turning to him, her big eyes wide and focused on
him, telling him to talk to her, then drinking in his
every word. He wanted her to stop looking out that
damned window at nothing and turn her attention
to him.

It was crazy. He felt like a young boy wanting to
do handstands to impress the pretty new girl in
school.

The pale wintry sun went behind dark gray clouds
and plunged the road into sudden darkness. It looked
like rain, with maybe even a little light snow. The
weather was very bad, even for November. The mete-
orologists were predicting a harsh winter. That meant
that feed prices would shoot up, not to mention heating costs. Cooper's thoughts fell into a familiar groove,

interrupted only when the woman next to him shifted. Immediately, his attention was wrenched away from his thoughts to her.

Maybe she was ready to ask him to talk to her now. He wanted her to stop thinking whatever it was she was thinking and smile at him. He was surprised at how much he wanted that. But she didn't. She just kept on staring out that damned window.

With a sigh, Cooper drove on into the gathering darkness.

Julia was startled out of her thoughts when Cooper pulled up to her house and cut the engine. "We're here," he said quietly.

She sat up. She'd almost gone to sleep during the ride back to Simpson. Julia felt slightly disoriented. The long drive, the silence and darkness had lulled her and it took her a moment or two to get her bearings. It had been so easy to sink into her thoughts as the cabin had darkened. Cooper, as usual, had been silent, but his silence hadn't bothered her. As a matter of fact, she'd found it restful. When she wasn't distracted by this crazy physical attraction which seemed to catch her unawares, she found being with Cooper soothing. She wasn't bothered by his silences. She thought she could detect the melancholy soul behind his strong, forbidding exterior. Something inside her felt certain that Cooper had hidden depths, perhaps of passion, if only he could unlock his feelings.

She turned to him. Half of his face was in shadow, the strong planes dark, almost exotic. She could see the faint gleam of his eyes in the dim light. Cooper's hand lifted from the steering wheel and for a moment, she thought he was going to touch her. The hairs on her nape lifted and her chest tightened.

He opened his door. "I'll get your things."

Cooper was unloading her book bags from the back before she could even answer. The man had driven her to Rupert, had kept her company, had carried her packages for her. She felt a real warmth for him as she walked up the rickety steps of her front porch.

She'd make sure she had a new cake recipe for Cooper to try when he came to pick Rafael up on Tuesday. Maybe a Linzer torte, or a plum cake. She dug in her bag for the keys, happily planning recipes. "Thanks for today, Cooper," she said, her voice muffled by her bag. "It was really nice of you to take me to Rupert." She started relieving him of her purchases. "So I guess I'll see you on—"

"I have to go out of town," Cooper's low, raspy voice interrupted her. "Tomorrow."

Julia stilled. Out of town? She looked up at him, no longer put off by his stern, unyielding expression. To tell the truth, having him around was kind of comforting, in an exciting sort of way. She stood staring at him, her arms awkwardly balancing the packages and felt suddenly chilled. "Oh," she said breathlessly. "Out of—"

"Town," Cooper said. "Until Friday."

"Well, that's . . . that's good," Julia said inanely, turning her face to the door and fumbling with the keys, hoping he wouldn't see her disappointment. This was so foolish of her, to feel as if someone had punched her in the stomach. The days until Friday stretched ahead endless and empty. And, of course she didn't even know whether she'd see him when he came back. *After all,* she thought, *what am I to him, anyway? His foreman's son's grade-school teacher.* Clumsily, Julia inserted the key and stumbled. Her books slid to the porch and thudded loudly on the wooden planks.

Julia and Cooper bent at the same time. Cooper's large hand covered hers and their heads met with a thunk.

Cooper lifted his head. His heated dark eyes bored into hers and she flushed hot, then cold. "Sally . . ." he rasped and she felt a rising tide of emotions she could barely identify flood her being. Fear. Loneliness. A desire so intense her skin prickled. Shame for feeling that desire. Her hands trembled.

Get into the house, she told herself, *before you do something crazy.*

Cooper was kneeling on the ground with her, his knees touching hers. Strong thigh muscles strained against the fine lightweight wool fabric of his suit pants and his shoulders were so broad they blocked out the view of everything but him. He was so strong, and Julia craved that strength with something that felt almost like pain. She was a heartbeat away from throwing herself into his arms.

She scrabbled madly to gather up her things, then rose to her feet unsteadily. "Thanks for driving me to Rupert," she said breathlessly. Cooper rose slowly, with the masculine grace that had her so enthralled. His face was stark, unreadable, all harsh angles. Julia was shaking and knew that she was going to do something very foolish very soon if she didn't go in *now.* She stepped quickly over the threshold.

"See you on . . . whenever," she called over her shoulder and slammed the door shut, pressing herself against the unpainted wood, heart pounding as if she had just slammed the door on wild beasts that had hounded her to her doorstep.

Cooper stood staring at the door, feeling tense and frustrated, damning himself for his upcoming trip to Kentucky, which he had planned four months ago. Something had almost happened here on this porch, and he didn't know what, but he did know he wanted to pursue it now. Not in six days' time. He wanted to pound on her door until she opened it and—and what?

Cooper stood on her porch for a long moment, raised fist an inch from the door, then blew out his breath in a white puff.

He turned and walked slowly back to the Blazer.

Ten

Julia couldn't fall asleep that night. She shivered as a gust of rain rattled the windows. Maybe the heating had gone off again, but she was too tired and too depressed—*too scared*—to get up and check.

Maybe Cooper would—Julia stopped herself. Cooper wasn't there.

Well, of course, he wasn't there.

He had a life, and things to tend to and a ranch to run. He wasn't responsible for a forlorn lady who'd had the bad luck to be in the wrong place at the wrong time. Why should he care what happened to her? If she had read too much into his helping her out, that was her fault.

It was time to get to know some other people in town. Everyone seemed to hang out at the diner. She might as well join them.

"Freshen your tea for you, Miss Andersen?" the young waiter asked Tuesday afternoon. His name tag said Matt Pedersen, and Julia wondered why he wore it, since everyone in this town seemed to know everyone else. And it was time for her to do the same.

"No thanks, Matt." Julia looked up smiling. "And the name's Sally."

"Sure, Miss Andersen, ah, Sally." Matt grinned. "Say—would you know if Coop's coming in this afternoon?"

Evidently everyone knew she and Coop were sort of an item.

"Cooper's away," Julia said between her teeth. She was idly doodling on the back of a school assignment. She watched a palm tree in a large terracotta pot grow on the sheet of paper in front of her. It had come from her subconscious, but it looked good. Inspired, she added a palm leaf stencil for the wall. "On business." She bent her head and concentrated on her drawing. "Till Friday," she added. She bore down hard on the paper and the point of the pencil snapped.

"Oh, that's right. To Kentucky." Matt nodded. "Coop's been planning that trip for months. Dad said Bernie told him that Coop was on the phone till midnight the other night, trying to call off the trip, but he couldn't." He angled his head curiously, trying to catch a peek at the sheet of paper. "Can I see what you're drawing?"

"He wanted to what?" Julia whipped her head up.

"Cancel his trip." Matt leaned forward, his eyes bright in the harsh light of the overhead neon strip. "Can I see what you're drawing?" he repeated.

"What I'm what?" Julia looked at him blankly, pencil still, mind racing. Cooper had wanted to back out of his trip? Surely not—not because of *her*?

"Sally?"

"Who?" Julia started and with an effort collected

her wits, which seemed to dim whenever she thought about Cooper. "What were you saying?"

Matt tugged the sheet of paper out from under her elbow. "What's this, Miss—Sally?"

"Oh . . . nothing. Just—" Taking a deep breath, Julia dragged her mind away from Cooper. "I like to doodle and I was just sitting here drawing the diner and I added a few things." She reached for the sheet, embarrassed. "It's nothing, really."

"I wouldn't say that." Matt took in the sketches of the stenciled walls, the small round tables, the tall plants. His blue eyes shone with excitement. "Really great." He looked around the diner, then back at the sheet of drawing paper. "This would really work here. Mind if I show this to my sister Alice? She runs the diner and she's been thinking about redecorating."

Despite herself, Julia was flattered. "Sure. Go ahead."

"I will. This looks great."

"What looks great?" Alice, a slightly older variation of her brother, wiped the crumbs off the table with a damp sponge, then sat down next to Julia and angled her head just as Matt had done. "What's this?"

"Oh, nothing much."

Alice pulled the drawing toward her, and studied it carefully.

"I was just, ah, imagining what the diner would look like if it were . . ." *nice.* Julia bit her lip at the last minute. "I mean, if—"

"You mean if someone had done something to it in the last thirty years?" Alice said.

"I didn't mean to imply—" Julia began, then looked at Alice who was watching her steadily with a half-smile on her lips. Julia had a feeling that the diner owner believed in straight talk. "Well . . . it *could* use a coat of paint."

"And a wrecker." Alice shook her head at Julia's automatic protest. "No, it's true. Mom never did anything to spruce the place up. She never made much money on the diner and then when maybe she could have afforded it, she got sick. Actually, I've been wanting to redecorate for a long time but . . ." Alice chewed her lower lip nervously. "I don't know much about it. It's really not my thing. Like cooking."

Julia tried not to smile, and then looked up as a shadow suddenly fell across the table. "Hi, Bernie. How's Rafael?"

"Sally." Bernie whipped off his Stetson. "Rafael's doing great. Thanks to you. I wanted to stop by and say that he's back on track now and we don't need to bother you anymore. And I also wanted to say that if you ever need anything, all you have to do is ask. We're—" He stopped suddenly, noticing the drawing on the table. "What's that?"

"Nothing," Julia said swiftly.

"What do you mean, nothing?" Alice asked indignantly. She pushed the paper around so Bernie could get a better look. "Sally's got a few ideas for redecorating."

"Yeah?" Bernie examined Julia's drawing with care, then looked around the dusty diner as if seeing it for the first time. "I'm no expert," Bernie said. "But it sure looks like it'll be nice."

"Yeah, it will," Alice said proudly. "About time this town had someplace nice to eat."

Bernie reflected. "You gonna fire the cook?"

Alice punched him. "I *am* the cook. You know that."

"Sally, you let me and Coop know if you need any help with this here redecorating project."

"That's awfully nice of you. Thanks." Julia looked at Alice's rapt face. She felt caught up in a river flowing toward an unknown source. "And thank Cooper, too."

"No thanks necessary. I reckon Coop'd do just about anything for you. And so would I." Bernie flattened his hair and put his Stetson back on, tugging at it in a sort of cowboy salute. "Sally. Alice."

He walked away, leaving Julia with her head whirling. What had she just gotten herself into?

Cooper was seriously annoyed by the time he made it to the diner late Sunday afternoon. It had been a harrowing week.

He hadn't even wanted to go to Kentucky, and had tried to wangle his way out of the trip, but Bill Rowland had insisted. And in the long run, it was probably a good thing because he *had* got a lot of business done.

Bernie had kept him informed in his nightly calls home on what was going on in Simpson. How Sally was helping Alice redecorate the diner and how Sally, Alice, Chuck, Matt, Glenn and Maisie were going to work on the diner over the weekend.

Cooper had been champing at the bit the whole time, frustrated that he wasn't there to help. There had been delay after delay, but he had finally made it to the ranch by two in the afternoon, had quickly showered and changed into work clothes and broken the speed limit into Simpson. It didn't matter because there wasn't anyone around to arrest him since

Chuck was at the diner. It was after three-thirty by the time he walked into the diner.

And there she was.

Cooper's eyes were immediately drawn to the tall stepladder in the corner. Sally was precariously perched on the top rung, arms outstretched to reach the top corner. She was doing something complicated with a roller. Cooper couldn't tell what, but the effect sure was pretty. The walls looked mottled, pale blue and white, like the inside of a robin's egg. Around the top of the wall near the ceiling, a pretty light-green leaf stenciling had been added.

Sally had haunted his thoughts and even his dreams during the past week. His heart picked up speed when he saw her.

He was a horse breeder and he knew all about the sexual pull the female had on the male of any species, horse or human. It had been a long time since he'd felt the pull, but he recognized it for what it was. It was sex, certainly, but also something more. He wanted to tell her about his week. He wanted her to redecorate his house—hell, redecorate his *life*—just like she was redecorating Alice's diner.

Cooper, stirred to the bottom of his soul, watched Sally up on the stepladder. She was turning the diner into a better and happier place, and he loved her for it.

And then because he wasn't a saint he was stirred by the pull of her jeans across her backside as she reached again for the top corner. She was slender, but curvy in all the right places.

It was so good to see her. Cooper stood a moment, trying to get a grip on all the unfamiliar emotions washing through him. One emotion was stronger than all the others. He'd never felt it before, but he instinctively recognized it for what it was. Rightness. A sense of homecoming. The feeling that he was where he was meant to be—here, with Sally.

She had fixed his broken window.

Eleven

When painting the diner started to tire Julia out, all she had to do was think of Cooper and she'd get new energy by imagining that she was slapping the paint all over him.

I'll be back Friday, he'd said.

Hah! she thought and vigorously pushed down on the paint roller, then eased up because she was spattering.

Who knew why she'd started waiting for him with a deep sense of anticipation already early Friday afternoon, when she and Alice and Maisie had started going over the plans? She'd looked up expectantly every time the diner door opened, only to be disappointed. Bernie, Chuck, Glenn, Loren, Matt, even her dog Fred had all crossed the threshold. And each time a man approached, her heart had leapt into her throat. And then sunk back to her heels.

All day Saturday she'd been in a state of expectant tension, making excuses in her head. *The flight was delayed. He has things to tie up at the ranch. He's been kidnapped by aliens.* A hundred times, she'd turned to Bernie, the question burning on the tip of her tongue: *Where's Cooper?*

She was a fool, reading things into Cooper's behavior that simply weren't there.

And what was so special about Cooper, anyway? she thought vengefully, as she dipped and rolled with unnecessary force.

Why should she care about him? He wasn't handsome and he certainly wasn't charming. He was—

"Cooper?" she whispered. She was reaching for the last bit in the corner up to the stencil wainscoting, when there he was at the bottom of the ladder—as if her thinking of him had suddenly conjured him up out of thin air.

He was looking stern, as always. With his dark skin, high cheekbones and midnight-black hair he looked a little like an Indian, and he'd sneaked up on her just as quietly. She stared at him for a moment, taking in his impassive features, wishing she weren't so glad to see him, when she realized that all the paint was dripping, destroying an afternoon's work. She lunged to catch the pale-blue drops and overbalanced. The stepladder tilted and she felt herself falling.

"Cooper!" she screamed.

"Right here." His voice was low and deep and calm as he stretched up and caught her by the waist. His grip was gentle but firm and Julia instinctively braced her hands on his broad shoulders. As easily as if he were lifting a can of coffee down from the shelf, he lifted her off the ladder and let her slide slowly down the length of his body.

Julia could feel his strength permeate her entire being. It was as if the world suddenly stilled and she and Cooper were the only people left on the planet

His face above her filled her entire field of vision. Her hands clutched his rock-hard biceps for balance.

Julia felt as if something had suddenly come into alignment, as if that missing piece from the heart of her world had suddenly slotted into place. With an almost painful jolt, she realized that she was falling in love with Cooper.

"You're back," she said breathlessly.

"Yeah."

She tried to read his face but couldn't. All she could see was that he was in the grip of some strong emotion. His eyes glittered and the skin was stretched tautly over his sharp cheekbones.

"When did you get back?"

" 'Bout an hour ago."

"I thought—I thought you said you were coming back on Friday." Julia knew that she should release Cooper's biceps and step back but she couldn't make herself do it. It felt so incredibly delicious to be held by him.

"Had an unexpected meeting. Flight was delayed. Had a hard time getting back."

"Well, I'm . . . glad you're back."

His jaw tightened. "Glad to be back."

"We're redecorating here, did you know?"

"Heard that. Talked to Bernie on the phone."

Julia smiled. She'd almost forgotten his laconic way of speaking. "I guess you left all your pronouns back in Kentucky," she said.

"Guess so." One side of Cooper's hard mouth turned up in a half-smile. Funny, Julia had never ready noticed what a beautiful mouth he had. Maybe because he didn't use it for much except looking stern. His large hands tightened on her and he stared at her for long moments, his gaze roving over her face, finally settling on her mouth. Then he slowly bent his head.

Julia could feel his body heat all over, she could feel his arms under her hands, his long thighs aligned with hers. She could almost feel the taste of his lips on hers, as her eyes started to close and she rose on tiptoe. A soft expectant sigh rose in the room . . . followed by a soft growl.

"Oof." Julia was knocked sideways as Fred who had turned out to be quite a protective sort of dog, launched himself at Cooper. Cooper kept his grip on her only long enough to ensure that she could keep her balance, then reluctantly released her and stepped back quickly, because what he really wanted to do was grab her and go somewhere, anywhere.

Someplace where half a dozen people weren't looking on with avid interest. At Cooper's glare, Chuck coughed into his fist and turned away and the others drifted off nonchalantly, pretending they hadn't been watching.

"Come on, dearie," Beth said kindly to a dazed Julia. "What you need is a good cup of coffee and some of Maisie's special double chocolate brownies." She led Julia to the kitchen and Julia followed her on rubber legs, knowing she needed a major sugar infusion to get the blood flowing back to her head.

Cooper stood rigidly in the center of the room, frustrated and half aroused, wishing he could just push some magical delete button and get rid of everyone in the diner. He turned at Bernie's hand on his elbow.

"Maybe you could brand her, Coop," Bernie said with a grin. "That way there'd be no mistake." He lifted his hands at Cooper's snarl. "Just a thought, boss. Just a thought."

"Well," Beth said a few hours later, placing her hands on her ample hips. "This is something else." She looked around approvingly at the changes that the past forty-eight hours had brought to the diner, which had a name at last. They had decided to call it the Out to Lunch.

Julia looked around, too, though most of the attention in her head was taken up with Cooper. Every time she turned around he seemed to be there, handing her a brush, mixing her paint for her, generally driving her crazy with desire. He'd managed to hold her hand, touch the back of her neck, run a hand along her back until she seemed to be sensitized, almost magnetized to his presence. She could feel his presence by the way the hairs stood up at the back of her neck.

"Hmm," she answered dreamily. Cooper was standing slightly behind her and she could feel his body heat. Julia was trying to act nonchalant but she trembled with the effort it took not to lean into him.

Beth gently nudged Julia's ribs with an elbow. "So, what do you think, Sally?"

Who? Her brain seemed to be mired in molasses. "What?"

"The diner—" Beth said patiently. "What do you think?"

"I—" Julia looked around and tried to focus. "It's great," she said.

"Nice." Cooper's voice rumbled at her back and set up vibrations in her stomach which reverberated throughout her body. Julia took a deep breath to try to calm herself.

Cooper was so close he could feel Sally's ribcage expanding and he cursed the fact that they were in the center of a room full of people. He wanted to take her hand and drag her off to her house, to his ranch, to a cave, but he couldn't. Maisie had cooked a celebratory dinner and had asked him if they could hold it out at the ranch, since he had the most space. It wasn't in him to refuse, though for the first time in his life he'd been tempted to turn his back on a good friend and neighbor. But he could try to make sure he drove Sally out and maybe stop the pickup on the way. Just for a few minutes. Though the way he was feeling, a few minutes weren't going to be enough by a long shot.

"Do you think you could do something with our store?" Beth asked Julia. "I mean, if you have time after school lets out and you're done grading papers or whatever."

"Your . . . store?" Julia asked, her senses quivering. Cooper had stepped even nearer. He put a large hand on her shoulder and her pulse went wild.

"Yeah. You know, make it modern or something." Beth waved her hand. "This is so pretty."

Despite the fact that Cooper was distracting her, Julia found herself interested. "Well . . ."

"Yes?" Beth said eagerly. "What do you think?"

"I'm not too sure you should go modern. Maybe you should turn your store into one of those old-fashioned general emporiums. You could repaint that long counter and put glass panes in to show the merchandise. And you could have the goods in barrels and canisters. And then—"

"Hey, everyone!" Chuck clapped his hands loudly. "Maisie's cooked us all a real spread and we're going out to the Double C to celebrate, so let's get going!"

There was a scramble for the door and Cooper tried to keep his hand on Sally, but she was waylaid by Beth asking for further ideas on redecorating the hardware store, then Alice was clamoring for her attention and he lost his hold on her.

They were out in the chill evening air, everyone making for their car. Cooper scanned the area for Sally and finally saw her wedged between Beth and Alice, getting into Alice's car. He caught her eye as she looked out the window.

"Plenty of time for that later, when we're all gone." Loren followed Cooper's gaze and grinned. He climbed into Cooper's pickup truck. "Now, Coop, what do you say about that new ordinance Newton's trying to get passed?" Cooper sighed, got into the driver's seat and put the pickup in gear.

"Oh, God," Julia said and closed her eyes.

"Good, huh?" Glenn asked proudly.

"Wonderful," she said reverently, and bit into the cold curried chicken again. "I had heard that Maisie could cook, and if this is any example of what she can do, then the diner's going to be a success."

"It's already a success, as far as I'm concerned," Glenn said, smiling. "I couldn't believe it when you suggested that Alice hire Maisie to be the cook. It got Maisie interested in something again. If the diner can't attract any new customers, then I'll buy forty meals a day just to keep them in business. It's worth it to me to see her smiling again."

Julia watched Maisie, a tall bony woman, as she

happily ladled out food from the buffet which had been laid out on Cooper's kitchen table. Even Cooper's table, with a surface area larger than her kitchenette back in Boston, could barely hold it all. Maisie had made enough food to feed a small army and every bite of it was delicious.

"I've got you to thank for this," Glenn said quietly.

"No, you don't," Julia said, surprised. "I didn't cook anything. It was Maisie—"

"I don't mean that." Glenn waved his hand impatiently. "I mean you're the one who gave Alice the idea of revamping the diner. Both Chuck and I are more grateful than we can say. If you ever need anything, anything at all, count on us."

"Oh, no really." Julia sipped her fruit punch to hide her embarrassment. She could feel herself turning red. "I didn't do all that much . . ." Her voice trailed off and Glenn turned to see what she was staring at.

Cooper filled the doorway. One of his workmen, a tall, lanky man named Jacko, had called him out for a problem as soon as they'd arrived and Cooper had disappeared. Now here he was, larger than life, peeling off his big leather work gloves, his dark eyes scanning the room until he found her. Their eyes met and Julia felt a deep tingle of excitement inside.

Cooper started crossing the huge kitchen and Glenn caught the glass of fruit punch which fell out of Julia's hand. Poker-faced, he set it on the table. "I, ah, have to go talk to someone," Glenn said. "About something. See you."

"What?" Julia turned to him blindly. "Oh, okay. Sure, that's fine."

He's magnificent, was all Julia could think as Cooper

approached her slowly, broad shoulders blocking out
the rest of the room. Moisture—was it condensation
or rain?—clung to his hair and Julia itched to run
her fingers through the thick dark strands. His expression was stern. She wanted to touch his face, see
if she could make the frown lines go away, trace that
hard, beautiful mouth with her fingers.

Cooper came up so close to her that she had to
tilt her head. He looked down at her and his face
had never seemed more harsh, more angular.

"Come with me," he said. "I want to show you the
horses."

"Yes, Cooper," Julia whispered, and put her curried drumstick down on the tablecloth, missing her
plate by a good ten inches.

Cooper laced his hand with hers and tugged gently.
It was only because he felt her hand so small and so
soft in his that he was able to keep from pulling her
after him and striding out to the barn with her in
tow. With a great effort, he managed to keep his
stride normal as they walked out of the house. He
felt like a stallion selecting a mare from the herd.

She even looked like a mare he'd once had, a
pretty little sorrel with delicate features and a lovely
arching neck. He had to remind himself that the sorrel had responded beautifully to patience. Sally probably wasn't going to respond to him dragging her
after him, throwing her onto the hay and biting her
neck like his stallions did when covering their mares.
But he felt that primitive, that possessive.

Despite his desire to take it easy, he had her running to keep up with his long strides by the time he
reached the barn. He yanked the door open, breath-

ing heavily, but when he stepped into the soft, musky, hay-scented darkness, Cooper's jagged nerves quieted instantly. The desire was still there, but tempered.

Like an equine chorus line, the horses lifted their heads one by one over the stall doors and watched him out of dark liquid eyes.

As Cooper led Sally down the long corridor, he heard a soft nicker and smiled. Showing Sally the stables had been an excuse, a rancher's version of come-and-see-my-etchings. But he really had wanted to show her the horses, he told himself. The beautiful animals were his pride and joy, and something he wanted to share with her.

"Come here," he said softly and put his arm around her waist. "I want to introduce you to somebody."

They walked in silence down the row until he stopped at the last stall and looked over the door. A gigantic horse with large expressive eyes looked back at him. Cooper realized that Sally wasn't tall enough to see over the door, so he fetched her a mounting stool. On it, she was almost as tall as he was. They dangled their hands over the door, shoulders touching companionably.

"Sally Andersen, meet Frontal System."

The horse was black and huge, with thick heavy muscles quivering under a shiny black coat. The stallion turned his head and fixed Julia with a stern gaze so much like Cooper's that she had to bite back a smile. "Well, he's certainly . . ." She stopped and turned to Cooper. "Frontal System?"

"Yeah." Cooper gave a half smile. "His owner has a sense of humor. He said that all black horses are named after weather phenomena—Storm, Lightning, Thunder. So he called his Frontal System."

"He's not yours?"

"No." Cooper made some kind of horsey noise in the back of his throat, and the huge animal moved slowly forward, a king deigning to greet his subjects. "I breed them, and then I train them. After two or three years, they go back to their owners. This one's due to be returned soon. Be real sorry to see him go."

"Oh." Julia could understand that. "Why is he doing that?" Frontal System's big black ears had pricked and turned toward them like antennae.

"He's not familiar with the sound of your voice," Cooper answered. "He's taking your measure. And see how he's bobbing his head?"

"Yes." The beautiful stallion's powerful neck was going up and down.

"Horses only have lateral vision, so he has to bob his head to increase his visual range. That's his way of getting a better view of you." Cooper swung an arm around her shoulder. "Basically, he's giving you the eye."

Julia laughed. There was something so comforting about being in the dark barn, the smell of hay mixing with the pungent smell of horses. Julia moved a little closer to Cooper. She stole a glance at him, at his strong profile, amused and a little touched by the fact that he seemed to be able to interpret the behavior of horses better than he could of people. Without stopping to think about what she was doing, she leaned over a little and gave Cooper a friendly kiss.

Cooper froze and when Julia saw his expression, she did, too.

She wasn't afraid of Cooper, but if there was any time to be frightened of him, that time was now. His eyes were focused on her with a sharp intensity. She could feel the tension in his big body as he lifted her down from the stool and stepped toward her. She took an instinctive step backward.

"Cooper," she breathed. "Cooper?" She hardly recognized him. The dark, friendly atmosphere of the stall had suddenly changed, becoming charged and sexual. She waited, heart pounding, for him to do whatever it was he was going to do.

Cooper planted two large hands against the stall door beside her face, effectively caging her in. He bent his head slowly, the intensity in his eyes so frightening that when he was an inch from her, she had to close her own.

Cooper's mouth fastened on hers and Julia was lost, plunged into a world of darkness and heat. Cooper's hands left the wall behind her, one cradling her head, the other around her waist, crushing her to him.

She braced her hands on his shoulders, feeling the solid muscles shift under her fingers as he drew her closer. Then, with a soft moan, she threw her arms around his neck, grasping in her hands his thick hair, still a little wet from the outdoors. Her mouth opened and as their tongues touched, she felt an electric shock go through her down to her toes. He tasted of darkness and danger and wildness.

His large hand moved up and down her back, then curled around her until he touched her breast. Julia tried to move even closer to him, to crawl inside him while desire pounded through her.

It was desire, but there was also someone pounding on the barn door.

"Coop!" Jacko yelled. "You in there?"

Cooper lifted his mouth. "No!" he yelled, without taking his eyes off her.

Julia was bent over his arm, trembling, and Cooper cursed under his breath as he took in her face. Her eyes were soft, her mouth wet and slightly swollen from his kiss. Not the only thing that was swollen. He was aching to kiss her again. Kiss her, touch her . . . he groaned. But not here. Not now.

"Come on." Cooper grabbed her hand and dragged her to the door. He felt like a wild man. His heart was pounding and his breath came in gasps. He yanked the barn door open and glared at Jacko, who backed off.

Two of his workmen and Glenn and Maisie were out in the yard, chatting, their breaths raising white plumes. Everyone turned to stare when they saw Cooper's face and said a few hellos, followed by silence. "We're just leaving," Glenn called out.

Cooper saw his pickup and made for it, pulling the door open and all but throwing her into the cab.

"Where are we going?" Julia cried.

Cooper slammed the door and pulled away with a squeal of tires. "To your house," he said tightly, "and to bed."

Twelve

She was shivering. Cooper could almost feel the air vibrate on the other side of the pickup's cabin and he felt ashamed of himself for having behaved like an animal. Moving slowly so he wouldn't frighten her, Cooper caught her hand and brought it to his mouth. Her hand under his lips was soft but cold.

"Scared?" he asked gently, dreading the answer.

Julia was touched at the tender gesture. They were on the last stretch into Simpson and the blacktop road was unlit. She could barely see Cooper in the faint glow of the instrument panel, but she could tell he wasn't smiling. And yet his touch had been soft and gentle. Every woman's dream man. Tough on the outside and soft on the inside.

She hoped.

Julia was feeling too vulnerable, too shaken. If she was making a mistake, it could destroy her. She was too alone and her defenses were low. His question echoed in her head. *Was she scared?* "No. Yes."

Cooper hated that. "Of me?"

"No." *Yes.* "Of the way you make me feel."

They were nearing her little house. The streets were deserted. Most of Simpson's inhabitants were still back at Cooper's ranch. Julia tried to understand what was happening inside her. Anticipation, excitement, maybe a little fear—fear of where this was leading. Not tonight but later. Julia had never felt more unsure of herself in her life. She knew where this was leading right now, at this very instant—Cooper had certainly made that clear. And it wasn't as if this were her first time. She'd had two affairs before; they'd been careful, civilized relationships where she had held the upper hand.

Nothing at all like what was going on here. That was it. She didn't feel in control here at all. She'd lost her self-control in the barn and even now, she could still feel his lips on hers, feel the recklessness in her blood.

Cooper drove the pickup into the side street and killed the engine. Total silence reigned in the darkness. He shifted in his seat and turned to her.

Julia was expecting him to pull her toward him for a kiss, a fierce one like in the barn, but he surprised her by cupping her neck with his hand. They sat there in the darkness, connected only by his hand. His thumb softly caressed the underside of her neck.

"Sally." His voice was a deep, disembodied rumble in the dark. "Do you want this?"

"Yes," she breathed and closed her eyes as he increased the pressure at the back of her neck, pulling her gently forward.

Where she had expected hot desire, he surprised her with the gentlest of kisses, sipping from her mouth carefully, as if she were a well of the purest springwater.

She murmured something, a soft little sound of surprise and pleasure and moved forward as if to say, *Yes, this is just what I want.* Cooper tried to fix that in his head as the desire rose like a mist to cloud his mind.

She wanted gentleness.

He lifted his other hand to the side of her face and deepened the kiss slowly, degree by degree. He used his hold to angle her head for a deeper kiss and felt her arms circle his neck. He lifted his head for just a moment and let his eyes roam over her fine-boned face. In the faint wash of light from the streetlamp, all he could see was pale skin and gentle curves. Her eyes were closed and her long lashes cast thick shadows over the curve of her cheeks. He touched her cheek with a forefinger, tracing the elegant line. Her skin felt like the warmest satin and she tipped her head into the caress. Helpless to resist, Cooper bent and teased her mouth open again with his tongue, his sharp desire colliding almost painfully with her need for gentleness.

She sighed and her arms tightened and he had to use all his self-control to keep from crushing her to him. She turned in his arms like water and opened more for him. The air turned hot and thick and he knew he had to stop right this second or they'd be making love in his pickup on the street, where anyone could pass by.

"Now," he murmured against her lips and broke the kiss reluctantly. "Let's go in now."

Julia pulled back, dazed and dizzy. Another fear rose up, stronger and more focused. If he could make her lose her mind with only a few gentle kisses, what would happen later, in bed? Not much later, when she could find the time to pull herself together, but right now, in a few minutes, while she was still unsettled and on edge.

It had been so long since she had been close to a human being. Held in someone's arms. Forever, it seemed. So long she could hardly remember how it was supposed to be. She felt shaky inside, her emotions too big, too scary to contain. Suddenly, the thought of what she was about to do made panic skitter up her spine. Maybe she should call it off, she thought, tell Cooper that she couldn't go through with it, but then it was too late because he was at the pickup door, helping her down.

She placed her hand in his and felt it close over her own, large and warm, and her heart gave a huge jolt. With a sigh of surrender, she gave herself up to the moment. Whatever was going to happen tonight was going to happen because she was being carried forward by the force of her own body's desire.

Cooper opened the door and Fred came bounding up to them. "Down, boy," Cooper said tightly and to her astonishment, the dog instantly dropped his belly to the ground and laid his head between his paws.

"How on earth did you do that?" Julia asked. "He's never—" Cooper's mouth descended on hers and she lost all thought. It was frightening, what he could do to her with a kiss. Julia felt herself falling, then realized that Cooper was carrying her into the bedroom.

His kisses were stronger now, feverish almost, and she could sense the hunger in him. It would have frightened her, except that she could feel the same fever, the same hunger, rising. She dug her fingers into his rock-hard shoulders and strained closer to him.

As in a dream, Julia felt the bed beneath her back, then Cooper's long, hard frame on top of her and she drifted as he kissed her with increasing fervor. He pulled away and she wondered why, until she felt cool night air on her skin and realized that Cooper was undressing her. She followed him up and feverishly pulled his black turtleneck sweater over his head and ran her hands over the smoothly muscled ridges of his ribs, and then the broad hard planes of his back. He felt so wonderfully good, so strong and solid.

"Cooper," she whispered and kissed his shoulder. His arms tightened around her, and he eased her back down on the bed, those large clever hands moving down her body, and with them came her jeans and panties. They had left the porch light on and by its faint glow she could see him next to her, naked, sitting on his haunches. Her heart jammed in her throat because she wanted this so much she was shuddering.

This had never happened to her before, this swelling ache in her body, as if all her cells were craving this one man. Cooper was motionless, his broad shoulders outlined against the faint light. She couldn't see his features, but she could feel the intensity of his gaze. "Cooper," she whispered again and held out her arms. He surged forward and Julia could feel the entire length of his hard body bearing down on her. His kisses were wild and she could feel his hard callused hands touching her neck and her breast. She cried out because the desire was as sharp as a pain. Then all individual sensations ceased as his hands and mouth roamed over her body.

He brought his mouth back to hers and held her face still as his tongue delved deeply. When he touched her intimately she moaned, and she opened for him. Her heart started pounding faster and faster as he shifted and settled over her until she could feel him probing, ready to enter.

Something, some last vestige of fear, had her clutching at his shoulders, but it was too late. Cooper entered her in one long strong stroke. Julia shuddered, then stilled. As if sensing her unease, Cooper lay still on her, in her, as she got used to the feel of him, the size of him. Then he began to move.

She cried out as the sensations became so strong she lost herself, existing only because Cooper touched her, loved her. The heat rose in the chill room. Cooper's mouth was locked with hers, his body part of hers as he moved within her, taking her passionately and completely, until with a soft cry he brought them both to a simultaneous climax.

Julia trembled from the aftershocks of pleasure and felt edgy, jagged, frightened at the intensity of what had happened. Her head swam and she could hear her own heart pounding, slightly out of time with Cooper's, while her head reeled. Her arms were still around Cooper's broad chest, expanding as his chest expanded with the rough breaths he drew in.

Please don't say anything, she thought. How ironic. She'd spent so much of her time begging Cooper to talk to her. But at that instant she couldn't bear the thought of him saying anything to her. Her emotions were too close to the surface for her to be able to control her thoughts, her words. There were things she couldn't tell him, but her secrets were all bubbling perilously close to the surface, just like her emotions. Tears pricked just behind her eyelids. She knew something important had just happened but she didn't know what.

He disengaged from her and gently rolled them until he was lying on his back. She was sprawled over him and he held her in silence as if he, too, didn't have words to express what had just happened.

Julia tried to calm herself by controlling her breathing as her yoga teacher had once taught her and soon she could feel her heartbeat start to slow down. She closed her eyes, resting her cheek against Cooper's chest, the rough curly hairs providing a touch of softness over the hard muscles. She drifted, then dozed.

She jolted awake, trembling and sweating. She tried to move but couldn't, because Cooper held her in a tight embrace. "It's okay, honey," he murmured, pushing back a lock of her sweat-soaked hair. "Just a bad dream. It's all right."

Julia's chest was hurting as she tried to breathe. Cooper was still holding her tightly. She inhaled shakily. Her face was pressed against Cooper's shoulder and she breathed in his scent of soap and man. The phone rang and Julia realized that this was the buzzing sound she'd heard in her nightmare. She pushed against Cooper's chest.

The phone rang again. Still groggy, she kicked back the covers with her legs.

Cooper's hands tightened on her. "Leave it," he said, nuzzling her cheek. Julia splayed her hands on his chest and leaned back as she looked at him. The lines that bracketed his mouth had deepened and the strong bone structure was accentuated. His dark eyes were more intense than ever.

The phone rang again and she gave another push at Cooper's chest, just hard enough so that he knew she meant business. His hands opened and Julia scrambled out of bed, wincing a little. Her body ached pleasantly from their lovemaking. She wasn't certain how she felt about what had happened, but her body did—it felt well loved.

Julia grabbed a dressing gown from the chair as she went into the living room, struggling into it while lunging for the phone before it could ring again.

"Hello?" Her voice was still husky with sleep and she cleared her throat. "Hello?"

"Julia? Julia Templeton?" Julia's heart gave a great thump as she heard her real name spoken for the first time in almost three months. Who on earth . . . Then a surge of panic swelled in her throat.

"Mr. . . . Davis?" she breathed. The U.S. Marshal assigned to her case . . . why was he calling her now?

"Yeah, that's right. Herbert Davis. Now, I want you to listen carefully, Julia. We think your identity has been compromised. We're not absolutely certain, but we're going to play it safe. From this moment on, I don't want you to talk to anyone, and I don't want you to trust anyone. Now this is what I want you to do—"

The phone clattered heavily on the table, falling from Julia's nerveless fingers. She could hear Herbert Davis's voice squawking from the receiver, a tinny remote sound. "Julia? Julia! Answer me! What the hell is going on? Julia?"

"Who was that?" a deep, raspy voice asked.

Julia gasped and turned. Cooper stood in the doorway, one powerful arm braced against the frame. *I don't want you to talk to anyone and I don't want you to trust anyone*, Davis had said.

"No one," she said breathlessly. She reached down blindly and slammed the still-squawking phone back on the hook. It bounced and lay slightly askew. "No one at all. It was . . . just a wrong number." Her dressing gown was gaping open. It was crazy, she and Cooper had just made love, but she pulled the gown around her tightly. Cooper moved forward and Julia took an instinctive step backward. Then another, until she bumped against the wall.

"Sally?" Cooper frowned. "What's wrong?"

Julia clutched the wall at her back, as if it could protect her. As if anything could protect her against Cooper.

In the dark, she had only felt him, felt the steely strength in his muscles. But now that she could see him, naked and powerful, he was fearsome. Julia could remember reading somewhere that the soldiers of ancient Sparta had fought naked to terrify the enemy.

Well, it worked. She was terrified.

He wasn't as lean-looking as when he was dressed. His shoulders and arms were heavily roped with muscle, powerful and frightening. It would be useless struggling against him if he chose to attack her. If he wanted to, Cooper could overpower her in one second, snap her neck the next and never break the rhythm of his breathing.

Cooper stopped in front of her. She stared straight ahead at the black chest hairs, at the deep indentation where his pectorals met, then slowly brought her gaze up. His face was tight, expressionless. A stranger's face.

Her lover's face.

Julia brought a trembling hand to cup his cheek.

She could feel his jaw muscles working under her fingers. His skin was warm, the beginnings of a beard barely apparent under her fingertips.

"Cooper," she whispered. A tear welled over and slipped down her face. "Cooper." She shook her head slowly, her eyes on his. "God help me, if I can't trust you . . . I don't want to live."

Cooper didn't answer. He merely held out his arms and Julia rushed straight into them.

Nature had expressly designed Cooper's shoulders for a woman in need. They were broad and warm and solid and Julia had never felt so comforted in her life.

"Do you want to tell me about it?" She could feel the vibrations of his deep voice reverberate in his chest. "I'm not much of a talker but I'm a hell of a good listener."

Julia took in a deep breath, the shock of fear still tingling through her system. Her head was whirling and she hardly knew where to begin.

She looked up at Cooper. From her vantage point, his cheekbones seemed more prominent, the lines of his face drawn with what she finally recognized as concern for her.

It wasn't a handsome face, but it expressed strength of character and honesty. She needed to tell someone and he needed to know.

It was time.

"My—my real name is Julia Templeton, and—" her voice hitched and she clutched Cooper's shoulder, trying to find the words to go on.

"And you're a redhead." His voice was slightly husky.

Julia blinked. "How on earth—" Then she followed his glance down to where her dressing gown gaped open and her cheeks turned pink. Of course he could tell she was a redhead. She shifted in his lap to pull the dressing gown closed, and felt his body's immediate reaction to her movements. The center of her own body, where he had been not half an hour ago, turned liquid. Her response to him was instantaneous and utterly beyond her control.

Julia wondered how on earth she could feel terrified, embarrassed and aroused, all in equal measure and all at the same time.

Cooper rested his chin on the top of her head. He nudged her with his shoulder. "So your name is Julia?" he prodded.

"Julia Templeton," she nodded, heaving a sigh of relief. At last someone was going to hear about the nightmare she'd been living through. "I'm—I'm not from Oregon and I'm not a grade-school teacher. I live . . . lived in Boston and I'm a book editor. Or rather I was." She straightened in his lap. "Last summer I decided that I was going to learn how to take artistic photographs, so I was happily wasting film in an industrial area along the docks. I came across this abandoned warehouse . . ."

Julia shuddered and with a cry buried her head against Cooper's shoulder. "Oh, God," she whispered, her voice muffled. Cooper tightened his arms.

"I had one of those automatic cameras, and I just walked around, shooting roll after roll. Finally, I walked into this inner courtyard and—" Her voice hitched. "I . . . I witnessed a murder, and it's all on film," she said simply and heard Cooper suck in a deep breath. She could feel all his muscles tighten.

"It was some gangland slaying. I was able to identify the murderer, a man named Dominic Santana. Apparently he's some big mob boss the FBI has been trying to get for years. I'm supposed to testify at the trial and they know he has a contract out on me. Until the trial, I've been put into the Witness Protection Program. That was my very own U.S. Marshal on the phone. Something's gone wrong with the security—"

"Idiots!" Cooper lifted her off his lap and surged to his feet. Julia stared up at him. Cooper was enraged, every line of his big body tense with anger. Julia felt a little flutter of something beneath her breastbone. Not fear, of course. She wasn't afraid of him, not exactly. "I had a few questions in mind about you, Julia. I'm just sorry this had to be the answer."

Something was going to happen and it was out of her hands now. In some hidden way, Julia had wanted to dump her problems into Cooper's lap and now she had. Quite literally. But mixed with the relief was trepidation because Cooper suddenly seemed charged. A huge, terrifying figure of a man, an uncontrollable force of nature.

A warrior.

"Cooper?"

But he wasn't listening. He reached for the telephone, pressed his finger on the hook, lifted it again, and angrily punched star 69.

When he heard someone say, "Herbert Davis" on the other end of the line, he snarled, "Who the hell are you, Davis?"

"Who is this speaking?"

Cooper tightened his grip on the phone, reminding himself to tighten his grip on his temper, too. "This is Richard Cooper. I'm speaking from Simpson, Idaho, from the phone of—" he shot a glance at Julia, curled up on the flowered sofa. She was still pale, her wide turquoise eyes fixed on him. She looked as small and as vulnerable as a child. The tactile memory of her soft, delicate frame still lingered in his hands and the very thought of anyone harming her . . ."I'm speaking from Julia Templeton's home. Now I'm going to ask this just one more time—who the hell are you?"

"I'm not authorized to disclose that information." The man's voice was distant, impersonal.

"You listen to me, mister. If you're from the U.S. Marshal's Office, then let me tell you that you're worse bunglers than I thought. I'd heard the rumors about how the office is going downhill, but this takes the cake. You send an innocent woman with killers on her trail out here without even an *agent* to watch out for her? What the hell kind of protection is that?"

"Ah—er—" Cooper could hear the man hemming and hawing. "We've been having some budget cuts and our Boise office—"

"Budget cuts be damned!" Cooper roared. "What's the matter with you people? You can't just dump a witness and hope she'll be safe. This woman needs protection. And by God, I'm going to see that she gets it! Starting now."

"Well, starting now she's not any concern of yours. We've got a leak in our security and we're pulling her out."

"The hell you are," Cooper said, his voice soft with menace. "You just try it."

"Listen, Mr. Cooper—"

"That's Lieutenant-Commander Cooper to you."

"Oh." There was a long silence at the other end of the line. "Navy."

"That's right. Navy. A SEAL. Retired, but I still remember a few tricks." Cooper smiled grimly. "And for the record, you're not taking Julia Templeton anywhere. She's staying here and you're going to deputize me."

There was a small shocked sound. "Absolutely not! Why I've never heard anything as outrageous as that in my entire—"

"You're going to deputize me, Mr. Davis. There's no way in hell you're taking her out of here. Not with the kind of protection you were offering."

"Look, Mr. Cooper, surely you realize that I can't trust you. How do I know who you are? You're complaining that we're not adequately protecting Miss Templeton. But we really would be bunglers if I just entrusted her to the first man who calls me up."

The man was making sense, damn him. Cooper clutched the receiver and stared at the wall, thinking furiously. "Okay," he said finally. "This is what you're going to do. You're going to call a number I'm going to give you. It's Joshua Creason's private number on a cell phone. You ask him who I am. I'll hold the line."

"This Joshua Creason," Herbert Davis hedged, "would that be General Creason, by any chance? You don't mean Desert Storm Creason?"

"No." Cooper raised his eyes to the ceiling. "I mean Joshua Creason the opera singer. Of course it's General Creason, you—" Cooper bit his tongue. He wanted the man's cooperation, not his antagonism. "You're wasting time."

Cooper was put on hold for several minutes. He leaned against the table, waiting.

"Yes," he said suddenly, straightening, and Julia's heart leapt up into her throat. Davis had obviously come back on line. "Uh-huh. He said *that*? He said he doesn't know me?"

Julia's gaze flew to Cooper's face. He gave a low laugh and scratched his jaw with a long finger. "Well, you tell Creason that the son of a bitch still owes me ten bucks. And that he better have improved his poker game." Julia could hear Davis protesting loudly and Cooper grinned. "Use my exact words."

Julia stared at Cooper, blinking. She stepped close to him. On tiptoe, she put her ear against the receiver and heard Davis relay the message. Even over two phones she could hear the roar of laughter, and then she heard another voice confirming Richard Cooper's record of Navy service, and up-to-date personal information.

Cooper listened carefully to Davis, saying 'yes' every few minutes. Finally, he hung up and stood tensely, jaw muscles working, lost in thought. When Julia timidly touched his shoulder he whirled to gather her in his arms, holding her tightly.

Overwhelmed, Julia put her arms around his broad torso, wondering what was happening.

"Looks like I've been deputized," Cooper said finally. Every muscle was stiff with tension and battle-readiness. "So that's that. You're staying here. The only way anyone will ever get to you will be over my dead body."

Julia drew in a long breath. "In that case, Cooper," she said faintly into his shoulder, "maybe you better put some clothes on."

Thirteen

"No!" Julia cried. "Absolutely not!" She jumped up and angrily paced around her living room.

The sheriff looked concerned, then pained.

Cooper had called Chuck Pedersen immediately and his friend had made it to her house in under ten minutes, huffing and puffing, which had given Julia just enough time to put on a pair of jeans and pull a sweater over her head. Chuck had walked into the house as Cooper had come out of the bedroom buttoning his shirt.

Julia had felt a quick flush of embarrassment but, to his credit, Chuck hadn't turned a hair. He had listened soberly as she had told him about the dreadful events that August day and what had happened since. Then both of them had listened as Cooper outlined his plan to keep her safe.

Julia grew more and more enraged as she listened to Cooper's low voice outline a plan that would have been condemned by Amnesty International.

The plan basically consisted of keeping her in a locked room with an armed guard outside the door for as long as it took the State of Massachusetts and the Federal Government to take the case to court. Julia felt sheer panic rise at the thought.

"That's not a plan, that's a prison sentence." Julia whirled and glared at Cooper. "You'll have to come up with something else, Cooper. I won't do it and you can't make me. I absolutely refuse to live under house arrest."

Cooper appeared unmoved by her outburst. He watched her calmly, his dark eyes steady. "You won't be anyone's prisoner. It's just that you'll be safe."

"I won't let you." Julia shuddered. Over the past few months, her teaching work, planning the revival of the diner, getting involved in the lives of townspeople—all those things had kept her alive and sane. She knew herself and knew how swamped with terror she would be if she were forced to stay holed up in a room. She would feel like a frenzied moth, beating itself to death against the windowpane. "You can't do this to me, Cooper." Her hands clenched. "You just can't. I think"—she drew a shuddering breath— "I think I'd rather die."

Cooper sat up, his eyes on her face. She sounded serious—she *was* serious—and his heart shot into his throat. He'd known fear, any soldier knew fear. Fear was useful—it honed your skills, kept you alive. But the thought of anything happening to his woman— and he had no doubt that Julia was his woman—terrified him.

"So what are you suggesting?" Cooper asked, frustrated.

"I'm suggesting we look at this reasonably." Julia tried to gather her thoughts. "What exactly did Davis tell you? Does he know for certain that Dominic Santana knows where I am?"

"No," Cooper said reluctantly. "But he strongly suspects it."

"On the basis of what?" Chuck asked.

Cooper turned gratefully to Chuck. At least Chuck could be counted on to be rational about this. "Julia's case information was in an encrypted computer file and someone got into it. The Marshal's Office hasn't traced the hacker yet, but they've assumed that your cover is blown."

The stark words hung there. Chuck looked thoughtful and Julia felt panic rise again, a dark fluttery sensation which threatened to cut off her air.

"So," Chuck said softly. "You're in real danger. As sheriff, it's my duty to protect you, Julia—and I have to cooperate with Coop."

"But—" Julia licked dry lips. "I understand there's a million-dollar bounty on my head. But there's no hard evidence that the mob knows where I am, is there?"

"No." Cooper spoke the word reluctantly. "But there's no guarantee that they don't."

Julia walked slowly to the window and looked out. The temperature had dropped and the ground had frozen. The uneven grass showed clumps of frost which gleamed a dull gray in the lamplight. The world looked cold and lifeless and Julia tried to imagine staring out this little window, hour after hour, day after day, frightened, lonely and trapped. At that thought, her heart turned as cold and as sodden as the ground.

Cooper walked up behind her and she could see his reflection in the dark window. She met his reflected gaze. "I can't do it, Cooper," she said softly. "I can't be locked up. Please don't make me."

Cooper felt as if she had kicked him in the chest. Everything he felt for her, every protective instinct in him reared up and shouted at him to keep her under lock and key.

He lifted his hands and put them on her shoulders. They felt soft and fragile.

"At least promise me that you won't go anywhere without telling me." Cooper felt her tense under his hands, then she turned around, hope flaring in her eyes.

Her eyes searched his. "I won't."

"Promise."

"I promise."

"You'll carry a gun at all times."

"I will?" Julia blinked, startled. "I've never used a gun in my life."

"You'll learn. I'll teach you. It's not rocket science."

"Okay." Julia tilted her head, considering. "And I want you to teach me the basics of self-defense."

"Good idea. Aikido."

"Ai . . . what?"

"Aikido," Cooper repeated. "It's a martial art. It doesn't require the physical strength of judo or karate."

"Yes, Cooper."

"You want to see one of your friends, Alice or Beth or Maisie, you let me know, and I'll accompany you. Either that or Jacko or Bernie will. I've got to tell Loren and Glenn, too," Cooper went on, shooting a glance at Chuck. "And the other men in town. They won't have to know why. All they'll have to know is that she's never to be alone. Not for one minute. And we'll arrange for a substitute to take over her class."

Chuck nodded.

Julia wasn't too sure what she'd bargained herself

into, but right now there was only one answer. "Yes, Cooper."

"You don't answer the phone. Ever. You let me answer."

"Yes, Coop—" Julia began, then stopped. "At all hours? What about at night?"

"I'll be here. I'm moving in with you."

"But, Cooper—" Julia's mind whirled. "If you move in with me, what about, I mean what will people here think? It's not really . . ." She shrugged helplessly and turned to Chuck.

"That's okay, honey." Chuck smiled and shook his head. "The very last thing you have to worry about is what people in Simpson will think. Everyone here likes you a whole lot. Hell, if anything, we're all really happy that Coop is finally getting laid."

Julia glared at both of them.

Fourteen

"Ooof!" Cooper rolled onto his left shoulder Monday evening. He was grateful for the mats he'd brought over from the school gym for Julia's daily aikido lesson. Instantly, she was on him, straddling his chest.

"I did it!" Julia crowed. She punched the air in delight. "I did it! I threw you!" She jumped up off his chest and did a little war dance around the room, knocking ferocious punches to imaginary victims.

"You sure did," Cooper grinned. He loved watching her happy and triumphant. He loved it when her cheeks turned that luscious pale peach instead of chalk white, when her mouth curved naturally into its normal expression, a smile. He stood up and winced. It wasn't easy throwing yourself, but it was worth it to see what a boost it gave to her self-confidence.

She had learned some basic holds, and he was beginning to be confident that she could fend off an untrained attacker. A *very weak* untrained attacker. But he wanted her to have the feel of a throw in her hands, to know what it was like.

So he'd thrown himself.

Julia was humming the theme from *Rocky,* jabbing the air like a heavyweight champ. She danced up to him, throwing shadow punches. "You're not so tough, big guy."

Cooper smiled and weaved. "Guess not. It's a humbling thought."

"I want a prize." She danced around him, in a teasing mood. "Otherwise I'll—I'll clean your clock."

"You've got me running scared." He couldn't resist her when she was in a playful mood. "Okay. Name it. Anything you want."

Julia stopped and looked up at him. "Do you mean it?"

He was feeling magnanimous. "Sure do. Anything you want."

"I want to go to Alice's Thanksgiving blowout at the diner tomorrow."

The smile was instantly wiped from his face. "No," he said. "Absolutely not."

"You said I could have anything I wanted. I want to be there when Alice and Maisie see how successful they're going to be."

"No." Cooper set his jaw. "Anything but that. You can have diamonds or pearls. You can have my best stud horse, but I don't want you in a Thanksgiving crowd. And that's final."

Suddenly the air filled with tension. Julia stopped her clowning and stood very straight and very still. She searched Cooper's impassive face. If there was one thing she'd learned about him, it was that he had a sense of fairness. "I worked days and days to renovate the diner. Alice is my friend now." She swallowed. Her voice was strained. "If I can't have friends, if I can't watch a friend's triumph, if I can't make plans, then I might as well not exist, Cooper. I migh just as well be dead. I'm asking you as a favor. I want to share at least a part of that day with Alice." Her eyes searched his. "Please, Cooper."

"Damn!" Cooper wanted to punch something. A wall. Dominic Santana. Herbert Davis. He knew exactly what she was asking and the danger it represented. It was crazy, foolhardy. And he also knew how much she deserved it and what it would mean to her. It wasn't right that she couldn't be there. *I don't want to do this,* he thought. *I don't want to say it.*

"Okay." The word came out reluctantly and he felt an oppressive heaviness in his chest. But it was almost worth that sinking feeling that he'd made the biggest mistake of his life to see her face light up. "Oh, Cooper, thank you!" Julia hugged him, then danced away. "Oh, I've been looking forward to it so much. I know how hard Maisie worked on the menu and it's going to be—" She stopped and eyed him warily. "This is a big concession on your part," she said.

"Yeah."

"We just had our first fight."

He sighed. "Yeah."

"And we survived it."

"Yeah."

"Though of course you are impossibly pig-headed."

Cooper's lips thinned. "And you are unforgivably reckless."

"And you forgive me." She smiled brightly at him. "Don't you?"

"Yeah."

Cooper reached out and pulled her into his arms. She lifted her mouth to his. Long moments later, she murmured, "I guess that means you really do care."

Cooper gave a rueful smile. "I guess it does."

"It'll only be an afternoon, Cooper," Julia said coaxingly. "Just a few hours. And maybe you could be there, too."

"Of course I'll be there." Cooper stared at her. How could she think otherwise? He'd be there, and armed. As would Bernie and Jacko. It was going to be as safe as he could make it.

"Well, I'm glad you changed your mind." She smiled at him. "It's nice to know that you're not always pigheaded."

"Thanks." He tried to smile for her. "I think."

"Cooper, talk to me," Julia whispered into Cooper's neck.

Cooper's eyes suddenly popped open. They had just made love and he was in that wondrous, relaxed place of body and mind that precedes drifting off to sleep.

Now he was wide awake.

What was he supposed to say? That the lovemaking had been spectacular? That he'd never felt this way before? That he was finding it increasingly impossible to contemplate life without her? He didn't have the words for any of those things.

He supposed that he shouldn't just drift off to sleep without a word after making love, but he was tired, what with looking after the ranch and Julia both. He tightened his grip on her, loving the feel of her slender ribcage under his hands, and stared at the dark ceiling, looking for inspiration.

"That's not very fair of me, is it, Cooper?" Julia said softly. She was closely snuggled against his long length, her body sated and replete, her mind ricocheting off the walls.

She seemed to be doing that a lot, lately. Her emotions swung wildly from one extreme to the other: fear so great at times it paralyzed her, mind-numbing pleasure, anxiety, contentment, sadness, joy. "I just can't get my mind to stop sometimes, you know? It just whirs on and on and I don't know how to—"

"I love you." Cooper's quiet voice dropped the little bombshell into the still night.

Julia's heart stuttered then stopped.

"I don't—" Her mind flailed about for a response while her body, entirely of its own accord, reacted to Cooper's large hand stroking her back. There was a long silence. "I don't seem to have a response for that."

"That's okay." His deep voice was even. "I imagine you don't. You're all tangled up now with what's happening to you. You don't know whether you're coming or going. You're far from home under a threat. And I have no business telling you something like that, especially now, except that I wanted you to know in case tomorrow—" Cooper hesitated. "Just . . . in case," he said finally.

"Cooper, I—" He placed a long forefinger against her lips.

"No. You don't need to answer me. Things are too crazy now for you to know your own feelings. Mine are enough."

Unbearably moved, Julia kissed his neck. "When did you get to be so wise?"

Cooper smiled ruefully in the darkness. "I may not be the most sensitive man in the world, but I'm not made of stone."

"No," Julia said thoughtfully, "you're not." She stroked his shoulder. She loved the feel of him, the strength, the sureness. When she was in his arms, he had the power to make the world and all its troubles fade away.

"I'm not made of steel, either," Cooper said on a yawn, "so cut that out. We both need our sleep." He splayed his hand over hers and pressed down, stopping her movement.

Julia laughed softly and shifted along his long, solid length. Cooper, her Cooper. No, he wasn't a man of steel. She'd seen him tired and worried and anxious. There were several new lines in his face and they looked permanent. She knew that she was the cause of most of them, but he had never once indicated in any way that he resented her intrusion into his life.

She tried to read her wristwatch in the darkness. She couldn't see the dial face, but it must have been close to eleven. Ranchers kept healthy hours. She hadn't had such early bedtimes since she'd been a child.

It was a starless night, the sky blanketed with clouds heavy with the snowstorm that all the forecasts were predicting. There was no sound at all outside the house. All the animals had hunkered down in expectation of snow, Cooper had said. She and Cooper could have been the only people in the world.

It was all so utterly unlike Boston. Back home, her neighborhood would still be alive with people spilling out of the theaters and cafés at eleven. Life never stopped in the heart of Boston; it went on around the clock. The late-night revelers on their way home

would meet the sanitation trucks and the office work-
ers trying to get an early jump on the day.

Outside her backyard here in Simpson was wilderness unbroken for fifty miles.

Such an odd place to find love.

Love. Cooper had said he loved her. She loved him,
too. Or at least it certainly felt like love. But surely
love required a sense of a future together? Some
sense of where they were headed? Julia wished she
could see into her future. Every time she tried to
understand her life, plan a little, a dark curtain descended in her mind. There was no future for her
that she could see, only the present with its terror—
and with Cooper by her side.

Suddenly, she needed for Cooper to know that she
cared. She lifted her head to tell him, but he pressed
her head back onto his shoulder.

"Sleep now, sweetheart," he whispered. "Tomorrow's Thanksgiving."

"Happy Thanksgiving, Coop, Sally," Alice said happily. It was late in the afternoon and the first flakes
of the snowstorm that had been threatening all day
were finally beginning to fall. Cooper put a hand to
Julia's back, and stepped over the threshold of the
Out to Lunch, dread pooling in his gut.

"Come on." An excited Alice tugged at Julia's
hand. "You've just got to see how we arranged the
vegetable platters. You'll love it. And Maisie made this
amazing sherry bread dressing. It's to die for."

God, I hope not, Cooper thought sourly as he relin-
quished his hold on Julia. He was reluctant to have
her out of touching distance, even if it was only to
follow a chattering Alice into the kitchen. He nodded

to Bernie, who got up and followed the two women through the swinging doors. Jacko remained where he was, at a window seat, his eyes sweeping the room, then tracking the street outside. Good men, both of them.

Cooper looked around. For the first time that day, he blessed the lousy weather. Very few people he didn't know had made it in for Thanksgiving. A proudly beaming Glenn sat with Matt at a table near the kitchen. At another table were three Simpson families seated as a party—the Rogers, the Lees, and the Munros and two couples Cooper recognized from Rupert, though he didn't know their names, and a young blonde girl who seemed to be a friend of Alice's.

He'd deliberately timed it so that he and Julia would arrive as the last of the customers would be leaving. He felt reasonably sure that there would be no dinner guests. Storm warnings had been going out all day. Only a madman or a fool would venture out in such isolated country after dark during a snow-storm.

For the thousandth time that day, Cooper regretted his impulsive decision to allow Julia to celebrate Thanksgiving here, and hoped it would be over soon.

This was the last time he was going to let her out in a public place before the trial. Davis said that the trial was scheduled for mid-January. After Christmas.

Cooper gave an inward groan. There wasn't any way he could stop Julia from wanting to celebrate Christmas with her friends. Julia struck him as the kind of woman who would consider not celebrating Christmas practically unconstitutional. Unlike him.

His past two Christmases had been normal workdays like any other.

Horses didn't observe holidays. They needed to be fed and watered and exercised every day without exception. And Cooper had several million dollars in horseflesh at the Double C.

Actually, it was becoming quite a problem trying to juggle everything going on in his life and Cooper didn't know how much longer he could manage. If only he could convince Julia to stay with him. A slow smile spread across his features, his first in a week.

That would solve so many problems. If he could convince her to stay over at the ranch it would be so much easier. He allowed himself a moment's daydreaming. Maybe he could coax her into doing a little decorating for him. Warm the old place up. Maybe he could even persuade her to stay on. Maybe, if he played his cards right, he could convince her to make the arrangement permanent—

"Well, it's sure nice to see you smiling," Julia said as she slipped into the seat next to him, adjusting her waist pouch. "I was beginning to think those frown lines were tattooed on."

Alice placed two enormous plates in front of them. "A little bit of everything," she informed Cooper. "Eat up." Cooper didn't recognize most of what was on his plate. Thanksgiving was turkey, sweet potatoes, cranberry sauce and pumpkin pie. Period.

But Julia seemed to know what everything was. "Mmm," she sighed, closing her eyes and breathing in the smells. "Sweet potato soufflé. Corn pudding. Turkey with raspberry coulis. Maisie's outdone herself."

Cooper dug in, though he had no appetite whatsoever. He chewed slowly, then with more interest.

Julia watched Cooper eat, secretly amused. Cooper obviously liked good food and, just as obviously, he hadn't had too much of it in his life. He thought she was a great cook. She wasn't bad, but hardly in Maisie's league. She took a bite of Maisie's stuffing and tried not to close her eyes in delight.

She'd been right to come. She'd known that Cooper would want to be with her and he needed this. He needed to let his guard down. He needed a little relaxation. She knew—though he hadn't said a word—that he was neglecting his work. He was turning himself inside out, trying to keep up the ranch and look after her.

Maybe she should offer to stay out at the ranch with him.

Though the idea would have horrified her only a short while ago, now it held a crazy sort of appeal. She could try her hand at redecorating his enormous house, have fun rattling around his seven-acre kitchen, watch Frontal System being put through his paces. But most of all, she'd have more time with Cooper. She could imagine them in the evenings, cuddled up around the hearth. There were probably twenty fireplaces in his house and they could try making love in front of each one.

Julia put another delicious bite in her mouth, fantasizing about fireplaces and Cooper when she started at a nearby noise. "What's that?" she asked.

Cooper put down his fork and reached into his pants pocket for his cellular phone. His jacket shifted and Julia caught sight of something dull gray and metallic under his armpit. He flipped the phone open and pulled out the antenna.

"Cooper."

"Cooper, Davis here. Listen, we've got a . . . a situation."

"I'm listening." Cooper's voice was low.

"I hate to say this, but it looks . . ."—Davis drew in a sharp breath—"it looks as if one of us has talked to Dominic Santana. My assistant, Aaron Barclay, took it upon himself to visit Santana in prison, and he knows Julia's whereabouts."

Cooper's hand tightened on the phone. He swore. "When was this?"

"Yesterday. One of our informants tipped us off. Santana got a call out early this morning." Davis's voice was dull with regret. "His killers are on their way. They might already be there."

Julia watched with growing dread as Cooper listened, his jaw clenching. His eyes went hard and opaque as he closed the cell phone.

"Cooper," she said softly. He turned his head to her, but he looked right through her. Cooper pulled a gun from the holster on his left side. "Cooper?" she whispered, scared now.

Cooper ignored her, his face tight. "Jacko," he called.

"Yo."

"Get Chuck."

"Right, boss." Jacko disappeared into the swirling darkness. Bernie took one look at Cooper's face and came over.

"Bernie." Cooper didn't look at up. He was filling the chamber of the gun with bullets he had taken from a jacket pocket. "Get the Springfield and the .38 from the pickup. Make sure you have plenty of ammo."

"Cooper." Julia tugged at Cooper's jacket. Her hand was trembling. "Tell me what's going on, for God's sake. What happened? Who was that on the phone?"

Cooper turned to her. "That was Herbert Davis," he said, his voice flat and cold. "Santana found out where you are twenty-four hours ago. His men are probably already here."

Fifteen

Everything seemed to happen all at once.

Chuck burst in, shaking the snow off his sheepskin jacket, carrying what looked like an arsenal. Bernie went out for a moment and came back in carrying several weapons. They both looked grim.

"Sally?" Julia turned at Alice's voice. "What's going on?"

A young, white-faced blonde woman came up to Alice. "Alice, what's all the commotion about? Those men have *guns.*" Alice put an arm around her. "I don't know, Mary. By the way, Sally, this is Mary Ferguson. She's a new member of the Rupert Ladies' Association."

"Hi, Mary." Julia smiled sadly. "This isn't the best time to meet."

"What's going on?" Alice asked.

Julia patted Alice's shoulder reassuringly, though she herself felt anything but reassured. "It's okay, honey."

"It's not okay." Cooper's deep voice from behind her made her jump. "Alice, there are some men on their way to Simpson. They're hired killers and they're out to get . . ." He hesitated a moment.

"Julia." She took a deep breath. What was the

point of keeping secrets any more? "Alice, my real name isn't Sally Andersen. It's Julia. Julia Templeton. And those men are after me."

"Are they now?" Alice said calmly. "Well, they're not going to get you." Alice looked up at Cooper. "Coop, what do you want us to do?"

Cooper looked around the refurbished diner, taking in all the details. His features were pulled tight with tension but his voice was as calm as Alice's. *I guess Westerners don't have panic genes,* Julia thought.

"Okay," Cooper said, "here's the drill. I want you to lock all the doors and dim the lights. Keep everyone in the center, away from the windows. Clear away all breakables. I'm leaving Bernie and Jacko here."

There seemed to be no question that Chuck would be going out with Cooper. The sheriff was overweight and over fifty, but Julia knew better than to question his decision. She also knew that Cooper had deliberately left his best men with her.

He'd be facing hired killers essentially alone.

Julia's throat tightened as she looked around. Alice and Beth and Maisie were busy clearing away dishes and shifting tables. No one had said anything to her.

It was her problem and everyone could have simply looked after their own skins and let her fend for herself. Cooper would have defended her—after all, she was his woman. But Chuck, Glenn, Bernie, Jacko, Alice, Maisie—it wasn't their fight, it was hers.

Tears stung behind her eyelids. The people of Simpson were laying their lives on the line for her without question. Julia felt a touch from behind and whirled to find herself in Cooper's arms.

She tightened her arms and breathed in Cooper's scent, pine and leather and man, trying to hold him so hard she could imprint him on her skin. A heavy ball of tears and terror settled in her chest. "Cooper," she whispered. "Be careful."

"Yeah." Cooper reluctantly peeled her away, holding her at arm's length. "We'll be okay." He searched her face. "How about you?"

Every gutsy movie heroine Julia had ever seen flashed across her mind and she did her best to give Cooper a brave, beautiful smile. "Yeah." She forced the sound out from a tight throat. "Yeah, I'll be fine."

"Get out your gun."

"Oh." Crazily, Julia had forgotten all about it. She pulled out the deadly little snub-nosed weapon, hefting it in the palm of her hand. She wondered if she'd ever be able to use it.

"Now you remember what I told you."

"Yes, Cooper." Julia blinked back tears.

"Present as small a target as you can. Lean your upper body forward. Pull, don't jerk. You have extra bullets?"

Julia pressed her ammo pouch and nodded.

Cooper gave her a brief, fierce kiss and was walking out the door with Chuck before her first hot tear fell.

The snow was falling in great gusting sheets of white. Already, a few inches covered the ground, softening footsteps, deadening sounds. Cooper crouched and made his silent way from door to door along Main, followed by an equally silent Chuck. Cooper's mind was racing. The U.S. Marshal had obviously felt guilty as hell that one of his own had betrayed Julia. As he should. Davis had worked hard to give Cooper as accurate a timeline as possible. Cooper reviewed what he knew as he flattened himself against the side wall of Glenn's hardware store.

Aaron Barclay had called on Santana after visiting hours at Furrows Island, citing a medical emergency. No phone calls had been allowed to prisoners on the island until seven o'clock this morning, when the records showed Santana placing a call to one of his underlings in Boston.

Davis had checked all the flights. Even assuming that a hit team had been assembled and ready to go, the very earliest the killers could have made it to Boise would have been by two this afternoon. All flights out of Logan had been delayed for four hours because of bad weather on the East Coat. It was a three-hour drive from the Boise airport to Simpson under fair conditions, assuming you knew the road. For men unfamiliar with the territory and in a snowstorm, it would take at least four hours.

Cooper checked his wristwatch under a streetlamp. Five thirty. He had about half an hour to set things up.

Cooper jerked and cursed when his cell phone went off. Before the second ring, he had it open and had cupped his hand around the receiver. "Cooper." His voice was low as his eyes scanned Main Street.

"Davis here. We've got news on this end."

Cooper closed his eyes and said a prayer. "Tell me the hunt is over and the dogs have been called off."

"Sorry." Davis sounded regretful. "I wish I could. What's happening over there?"

"I've secured Julia as best I could. Now the sheriff and I are going over to her house to prepare the welcoming committee."

"Well, good luck." Davis's voice sounded tinny.

"Tell the bad guys they'd never have collected anyway."

"What the hell does that mean?" Cooper snarled into the phone. He was taking his fear and anxiety out on Davis, but the man deserved it. If the marshal had been watching his back and doing his job right, this would never have happened.

"Santana's dead."

"What?" Cooper remembered at the last minute to keep his voice low. Snow muffled sounds, but he couldn't afford the slightest mistake. Not with Julia's life at stake. "Run that one by me again."

"Santana suffered a massive coronary around three." Not even the heavy static could hide the rich satisfaction in Davis's voice. "He was pronounced dead at three thirty p.m. Eastern Standard Time. I just heard about it."

"Could he be faking it?"

"Not unless he's got a special arrangement with God. Santana's vital organs are being inventoried on an autopsy table right now. So, if you catch these guys, it's all over."

"Save a piece of Santana's hide for me," Cooper growled, "I want to nail it to my wall." He switched the phone off and put Davis's news in a far corner of his mind. He couldn't afford any distractions. He had to focus his entire attention on the mission at hand.

"Who was that?" Chuck's voice was the merest breath in his ear.

"Later." Cooper's voice was just as low. He pointed to Julia's corner house and pointed to indicate the back entrance. Chuck nodded. They made their way silently around the house and Cooper let himself in with his key. Moving quietly, efficiently, he pulled a Maglight from his pocket, a small stun explosive and a trip wire from the satchel. He also pulled out the towels he'd stuffed into his satchel and gave one to Chuck.

"Dry off," he whispered. "Can't leave any tracks." Chuck nodded and dried his shoes while Cooper fixed the explosive device to the door handle. One turn of the handle and the noise and flare would disable a man for at least ten seconds, long enough to get a jump on him—or them.

After a few moments, the setup was ready. Cooper grunted with satisfaction and moved quickly into the bedroom.

He was stuffing some of Julia's clothes under the blanket to make it look as if she were taking a nap in case someone were to look through her window, when he felt Chuck's hand on his shoulder. He nodded. He'd heard it, too. A car, coming down East Valley Road.

Cooper checked out the window. The car was traveling without headlights. It came to a gliding stop about fifty yards from the house and two figures got out.

Cooper pulled Chuck into the closet and pulled the door closed. That should protect them from the worst of the stun blast.

Cooper checked his watch. The men were fifteen minutes early on Davis's earliest estimate. These guys were fast and they were good.

But he was better.

Julia heard the explosion from three blocks away. The windowpanes of the Out to Lunch rattled briefly, then there was utter silence, which seemed to find its echo in the sudden void in her chest.

Julia looked around and saw shocked faces, except for Jacko and Bernie. Their faces were grim, their weapons held at the shoulder and cocked.

"No," Julia whispered. Alice stared at the floor and Maisie moved forward to put her arms around Julia's shoulders. Julia pushed her and her sympathy away with stiff arms. "No," she said, louder.

No one said anything.

With numb fingers, Julia checked the barrel of her gun for the thousandth time. She realized suddenly that if anything had happened to Cooper, she'd have the nerve to use it. She clicked the safety off and bolted out the door so quickly she got past Bernie and Jacko. "Hey!" she heard Bernie yell, "Coop said—"

But by then she was out on the street. She didn't want to hear from Bernie what Cooper had said. She wanted to hear it directly from Cooper. She wanted Cooper himself to scold her and complain about her lack of obedience. She wanted Cooper to chew her out, tell her she'd put herself in danger, and that he wasn't going to tolerate it. She wanted Cooper . . . she wanted Cooper. Alive.

Julia ran toward her house, wiping tears and snow out of her eyes, slipping a little in the snow, which reached almost to her ankles. It could have reached her chest and she wouldn't have noticed or cared, because all she wanted to do was get to Cooper.

She ran and slid the last few feet before her gate, then tore up the rickety steps and slammed the door open. She stood, panting and wide-eyed, in her gunman's crouch as she took in the scene.

Two sullen men were sitting on the floor, handcuffed, with their backs to her living room wall. Chuck was reading them their rights in a monotone, every paunchy inch the small-town sheriff again. Cooper walked in from the bathroom sucking his reddened knuckles, a heavy scowl on his face.

Julia's heart gave a great lurch and her voice tried to make its way through her throat. Shaking, she put the safety back on the gun and set it down on the coffee table. "Cooper—" Nothing came out and she tried again. "Cooper." Her voice was reedy and weak, but he heard.

He turned, still frowning, and frowned even more when he saw her. "What the—" he began, then looked past her. "Bernie, I thought I told you to keep her safe."

Bernie opened his mouth to answer, but he was out of breath. It didn't make any difference, anyway, because Julia had launched herself into Cooper's arms with a cry of joy. "Oh, Cooper, when I heard the explosion, I thought, I thought—"

"I know." Cooper hugged her tightly. "Listen, I thought I told you to stay put."

Julia couldn't talk. She simply nodded into his shoulder.

"I told you to stay put, didn't I? That wasn't asking too much, was it? You were supposed to stay right where you were until I came back to get you."

Julia nodded, shook her head, then laughed. She pulled her head back from his shoulder. "I'm glad to see you, too." It was so wonderful to feel him, his strength, his solidity, even his scratchy jacket that smelled of wet wool. She stilled and stared at the two men slumped against her wall. Disengaging herself from Cooper, she walked over and looked down.

"What happened to their faces?" she asked.

"Walked into a door," Cooper said quickly.

"Resisted arrest," Chuck added.

Julia studied the battered faces of the enemy. One man was blondish, with a long, dirty ponytail and the other was dark, with a crewcut and an earring. But no matter the superficial differences, they shared a look. The same look that Santana had. That kind of face, cold, cruel, brutal, was stamped into her memory. She knew with a sickening certainty that they would have killed her without a second thought.

And Santana still would.

She turned, the thought rousing in a heartbeat all the sheer terror she'd felt over the past few months, compounding it and running it through her veins. "Cooper." She put a hand to the wall to steady herself. "Cooper, Santana knows where I am now. He can send others—"

"Santana's not going to be sending anyone anywhere," Cooper answered. "He's dead, honey. He died a few hours ago. Heart attack. The nightmare's over."

It took a second or two for the words to penetrate. The nightmare was over. She let the words roll around in her head. The nightmare was over. "Oh," she said inanely. "Oh that's . . . that's good."

Cooper looked at her, frowning. "Sit down, honey." When she shook her head, he walked her over to the armchair and exerted gentle pressure. "Sit down before you fall down."

She didn't want to obey him, but her knees buckled.

Julia felt a deep tremor start from within, like the precursor to an earthquake. Dots swam in front of her eyes and she tried to focus. Her mind was finding it hard to absorb what Cooper had just said.

The nightmare was over.

Three months of agonizing fear, of isolation and exile. Three months of waking shuddering and sweating from sleep only to find that the waking terror was worse than the terror that stalked her in her dreams.

The nightmare was over.

A great sob was wrenched from her chest, then another. "Oh, God," she gasped, dazed, the enormity of it striking her all over again. She could hardly fathom it, could barely catch her breath, could hardly get her mind around the thought. Cooper took her trembling hands in his and she stared blindly at their linked fingers. "It's over. I don't have to stay here anymore. I can do what I want. I can go home. Oh dear God, I can go home again. I can't wait. Oh, God, I can't wait. I want to go home *now.*" Tears were leaking out of her eyes and her heart was thumping wildly in her chest. Julia barely noticed when Cooper released her hands.

She raked her trembling hands through her hair and thought—*home.* She raised her head on a deep, calming breath, letting the idea run through her mind once again, as if struck anew. It was over.

The nightmare was over.

She looked around and focused on Cooper, watching him retreat. Chuck was retreating, too. Bernie had turned his back and was standing stiffly by the door.

All of a sudden, she remembered what she'd said and it struck her how Cooper would take it. He thought she meant that she wanted to go home and never come back. But she hadn't meant that—not at all. What she'd really meant was, she'd meant—she didn't know what she'd meant.

Julia tried to gather her thoughts but it didn't work. It only made her head hurt.

She realized now how far she'd come in understanding Cooper, how well she had learned to read his face, because all of a sudden she couldn't read anything at all. He stood before her, straight and tall, his face an impenetrable mask.

Chuck was herding the two shackled prisoners out the door. Bernie had already left. Cooper had one hand on the doorjamb.

"You won't be bothered again." Cooper's voice was as remote as his face. "Davis said that he'll call you in for a deposition, but it won't be anytime soon. I'll book you a flight out tomorrow. One of my men will take you to the airport."

"No, I—" Julia stretched out a hand. She couldn't stand to see that blank look on Cooper's face. She bit her trembling lips and let her hand drop.

There was so much she wanted to say to Cooper, but it looked like she wasn't going to have the time because he was out the door and past her gate before she could get her leaden feet to stir.

Maybe it was better this way. There was no way on earth that she could explain anything to anyone, not tonight, certainly not right now. Julia sank back onto her couch. The horrendous little couch with the ugly cabbage roses.

It struck her that she was going to miss those stupid roses. Her own couch in Boston was covered in an exquisite beige chintz, but these roses, as ugly as they were, had . . . character.

There were a lot of things she was going to miss.

She was going home. For the first time, Julia allowed herself to savor that thought. Home.

But what did she have there? What was home now? What was waiting for her? Her job? Since Warwick Publishing's takeover by a larger corporation, editors had been assigned one stupid project after another, with little chance for advancement. There wasn't anything she really wanted to return to.

Except her Boston friends.

But Julia suddenly realized that all the time she'd been in Simpson, she hadn't wondered how they were. She and Jean and Dora had got along reasonably well together at the office, read the same books and occasionally met on Saturdays for coffee and gossip. That was all.

It wasn't like here, where she was intimately involved in the daily lives of her new friends. She wanted to know what Alice would be doing, if the Out to Lunch would be a success. She wanted to go on trying out Maisie's wonderful recipes. Matt had mentioned that he had written twenty pages of a sci-fi epic and she wanted to read it. She couldn't leave them.

Julia started at the wet muzzle laid adoringly on her knee. And Fred needed her. She couldn't leave Fred.

She couldn't leave Cooper.

It had been the emotion and relief of the moment that had made her react that way, but the fog was beginning to clear. She wanted Cooper back—*her*

Cooper, who made her feel safe and excited all at once.

She was calmer now—and resolute.

She'd been foolish, but that was okay. Cooper would forgive her. He had to or she'd—she'd beat him up. They'd had a mock fight during her aikido lesson and she'd managed to throw him to the floor.

Some martial arts expert.

Well, if he had his stupid pride, she didn't. Julia stood up, grateful her knees were finally steady.

She picked up the phone and stared at it. There was no dial tone. She shook it as if that would give her a signal. The phone rang, startling her and she dropped the receiver, then frowned at it. It rang again and she realized that it was the doorbell ringing and not the phone.

Whoever it was would have to go away because she didn't want to talk to anyone but Cooper right now.

Julia opened the door. A young blonde woman stood on her doorstep, shoulders covered in snow, clutching a briefcase. Julia frowned, then suddenly remembered. Mary Ferguson.

"Hi, Sally." Mary smiled timidly. "Listen, I'm leaving before the snowstorm gets worse. Alice was telling me how much help you'd been in redecorating the Out to Lunch, and then Beth was saying you were helping her . . ." She shifted uneasily on the doorstep and shivered. "I know you've been through a lot but I was wondering whether you'd look at the floor plan of this office I was thinking of renting? It would just take a few minutes of your time."

Mary definitely wasn't Cooper. Julia wanted her to go away. Good manners warred briefly with her desire to run after Cooper and good manners won by a hair.

She'd look at the plans, give Mary a quick opinion, say goodbye and *then* go run after Cooper.

"Sure." Julia smiled wanly and stepped back. "Come on in."

"That was some excitement we had this afternoon," Mary said. She put her case on the floor. "I was scared to death."

"Yeah." Julia went into the kitchen to put some water on to boil and came back holding two mugs. "Am I glad the whole thing is over."

"Well, that's the thing, Julia Templeton," Mary said regretfully. "I'm afraid it isn't over at all."

Julia could barely hear the sound of the mugs shattering over the pounding of her heart.

Mary Ferguson was holding a gun, pointed right at her.

Cooper regretted leaving Julia almost as soon as he was out of town. His pickup bucked over a hillock of snow and he fought fiercely for control of the wheel.

Even the wind wanted him to turn around and go back.

Pride was a funny thing, he mused. Cooper men had been choking on their pride for four generations. But pride didn't make you laugh or explain to you how human beings worked or warm your bed at night. Pride made a very cold companion.

So she'd said she wanted to go home. Big deal. Of course she wanted to go home. Anyone would. He hadn't even given her a chance to say anything. He hadn't allowed for the aftermath of shock and fear. No siree. He'd just coldly informed her that she'd be accompanied to the airport.

Cooper could imagine Julia now, forlorn and shaken from the day's events. He could just see her, curled up in a small ball on that ridiculous, lumpy couch in her rented house. Now, of all nights, she shouldn't be left alone. He could kick himself for his behavior.

The pickup bucked again and Cooper slowed. All of a sudden, he couldn't wait to get back to her. He fished for his cell phone to tell her that he was turning back. He dialed her number. There was no answering ring.

He must have dialed a wrong number. Cooper stopped the pickup and punched Julia's number again, frowning. He tried three more times, then switched the phone off. Fear such as he had never known before seized his innards.

His pride had been hurt and he hadn't been thinking straight and he cursed himself.

Nobody had said that Santana had only sent two killers. Another one could easily have been dropped off as a backup before arriving at the house. A killer could be in her house right now. And he had left Julia alone and defenseless.

While ice ran in his veins, Cooper wrenched the steering wheel of the pickup, backed into a snowbank and turned around. Cursing himself for a fool, he pressed the accelerator and sped through the swirling night.

"Um, Mary." Julia licked dry lips. "You want to be careful with that . . . that gun. It might be loaded."

"Of course it's loaded, you fool." Mary reached into her case and brought out a camera, setting it down on the coffee table. "And there's a bullet with your name on it that's been waiting for three months now." She eyed Julia critically, dispassionately. "Move against that wall over there. I need a white back-drop."

"Mary," Julia whispered. "What are you doing?"

"Doing?" Mary stared at her. "I'm earning a mil-lion dollars. What do you think I'm doing?" She waved the gun. "Now move."

Julia shuffled in the direction Mary indicated, watching her. She sidled by the coffee table where her weapon was.

"Ah-ah, Julia. I noticed you had a gun." Mary reached for the weapon, flicked open the chamber and emptied it. "A Tomcat .32. Someone very smart has been advising you, Julia. Not that it's going to do you any good."

Why had she ever thought that Mary was young? The woman must be a genius with makeup. Now that she was looking carefully, Julia could see the fine lines around the eyes, the creases from nose to mouth.

"Mary," she whispered. "Please don't do this."

Mary laughed. "First of all, my name isn't Mary, not that I have any intention of telling you what my real name is. Secondly, of course I'm going to do it. I've been tracking you since August. You're going to get me a million dollars. Or rather your head is." Mary bent over to check the lens of the camera, then walked around the living room, turning on all the lights. The whole time, her gun was trained on Julia. "The light has to be just right," Mary murmured.

"But—" Julia's mind whirled, trying to take in what was happening. "They took Santana's men away. He tried to get me, but it didn't work."

"Those goons?" Mary's face grew pinched and

white and Julia realized that the emotion she'd seen in Mary's face in the diner had been rage and not fear. "Two-bit hired guns. That's all they were. And to think they almost cheated me out of my money. But with these snapshots, Santana will know who he has to pay—"

"He won't!" Julia almost sobbed with relief. "Santana won't pay you. He can't. Haven't you heard? Santana's dead. He died this afternoon."

"You're lying!" Mary snarled. "I'm going to shoot you and send Santana the snapshots. And then he'll transfer the money into my offshore account."

Startled, Julia looked into Mary's pale blue eyes. She didn't see the cold brutality of Santana or the two thugs who'd broken into her house. All she saw was the flat, blank stare of madness.

"But he can't! He can't send you any money." Julia tried desperately to get through to her. But Mary seemed impenetrable and utterly unreachable. The gun in her hand began its slow trajectory upward.

Time! Julia thought wildly. She needed more time. If only she could do something—delay Mary until someone could come for her. Surely Cooper—but she'd sent Cooper away. Stupidly, stupidly, she'd sent Cooper away.

The gun was aimed at her heart now, her wildly thudding heart. "Please," she whispered.

"Please what, Julia?" Mary mocked. "What on earth can you offer me that can top a million?"

"You won't get the money, Mary," Julia said reasonably. "And you won't get far in this snowstorm, either. They'll catch up with you, and all for nothing, Mary. All for nothing because there isn't anyone to give you the money. Santana is dead."

"You *lie!*" Mary screamed and pulled the trigger.

Julia was slammed against the wall and a fiery pain erupted in her shoulder. She stood, wavering, until her legs collapsed. A flare went off in her eyes and then another. It took her a moment to realize that it was the flashbulb of the camera.

Mary's shoe slipped a little in the blood and a look of disgust crossed her face. "Blood," she grimaced, "I hate blood. Now just a few more snapshots, and then the last shot—the head shot—and we'll be all done. Then I have to go. I've got a plane to catch."

Julia watched the front of her sweater turning red and realized dimly that it was her blood turning her sweater red. She heard a low, vicious growl that penetrated the fog clouding her mind.

"Damn it!" Mary kicked at Fred, who was standing in front of Julia, hackles raised. He snarled and snapped at Mary's hand as she tried to put the muzzle of the gun against Julia's temple. The dog bared his teeth and gave another hair-raising growl. "Call this stupid mutt off," Mary hissed. "I've got to get out of here."

"Nice doggie," Julia murmured. "Good Fred." There was pain now. Waves of it. Starting from far away, but coming closer.

"Well, if you won't call him off, I'll just have to do it from here." Mary sighted down the barrel at Julia and closed one eye.

Julia's head felt as if it weighed a thousand pounds. She lifted it with difficulty and stared down the gun barrel pointed straight at her forehead.

She didn't want to die. She wanted to live. She wanted to live and marry Cooper and give him a houseful of redheaded girls who would drive him crazy. And she'd never even told Cooper she loved him.

Julia watched Mary's finger tighten and thought—this is it.

Then, there was a loud noise and Mary collapsed in a silent heap. Fred barked wildly as Cooper kneeled beside her, tearing off his jacket and stuffing it against her shoulder, cradling her in his arms, shouting, "Julia, Julia!" She could feel his hands running over her, checking for injuries, then he pressed down strongly on the wound on her shoulder.

Pinwheels exploded behind her eyes and she wanted to tell him to cut it out, but the pain took her breath away.

"Julia." Cooper lifted her carefully. His deep voice cracked. "Don't die on me, Julia. I need you. Just hold on. We'll get a Medevac copter and get you to the county hospital. Talk to me, Julia. You can't die. I love you. Talk to me, please."

Talk to me. Where had she heard those words before?

"Hey," Julia whispered. She reached out with a trembling hand and cupped his cheek. It was warm and rough and solid, just like Cooper. "That's my line."

Six months later . . .

"Now what's my line?" Julia whispered. Cooper glared at her. He looked unbelievably handsome in black tie and black cowboy boots.

"Don't you know?" he hissed back.

"You're the one who's done this before."

The minister smiled benevolently at them, and a few of their friends who were close enough to overhear couldn't conceal smiles of their own.

"You're supposed to say I do."

She grinned up at him, and lifted up her veil. Would Coop *ever* be able to take a joke? Well, maybe not on his wedding day.

"I know," she said sweetly. "And do I ever!"

ABOUT THE AUTHOR

Elizabeth Jennings is a born wordsmith and roman-
tic. Her day job—until she can publish enough Precious Gems to become a millionaire—is simultaneous
interpreting and translating. The loves of her life are
her husband, Alfredo, and her son, David. She lives
in Italy, land of sunshine, magnificent architecture,
wonderful food and bad postal service. She welcomes
comments from readers at acinnella@hsh.it.